Mother screamed when she took the lid off a pot in the kitchen. Inside, dozens of fat, hairy caterpillars bobbed up and down in a kind of soup. They smelled disgusting. Mother took a deep breath and slammed the lid back on the pot. "We mustn't criticize Uncle Zeka," she told Tapiwa. "The people where he lived were so poor they didn't even have chickens. Tsetse flies and disease killed everything. They had to eat whatever they could find. I wish, though," she said half to herself, "that he would simply eat what I cook and not try to help out."

That night Uncle Zeka served his caterpillar stew, but no one wanted it. "I'm sorry," said Father. "We aren't used to this kind of food."

"You're missing a good thing," said Uncle Zeka, helping himself to a large bowlful.

Do You Know Me

NANCY FARMER

illustrated by Shelley Jackson

PUFFIN BOOKS

PUFFIN BOOKS
Published by the Penguin Group
Penguin Books USA Inc., 375 Hudson Street, New York, New York 10014, U.S.A.
Penguin Books Ltd, 27 Wrights Lane, London W8 5TZ, England
Penguin Books Australia Ltd, Ringwood, Victoria, Australia
Penguin Books Canada Ltd, 10 Alcorn Avenue, Toronto, Ontario, Canada M4V 3B2
Penguin Books (N.Z.) Ltd, 182-190 Wairau Road, Auckland 10, New Zealand

Penguin Books Ltd, Registered Offices: Harmondsworth, Middlesex, England

First published in the United States of America by Orchard Books, 1993
Reprinted by arrangement with Orchard Books, New York
Published in Puffin Books, 1994

5 7 9 10 8 6

Text copyright © Nancy Farmer, 1993
Illustrations copyright © Shelley Jackson, 1993
All rights reserved

LIBRARY OF CONGRESS CATALOGING-IN-PUBLICATION DATA
Farmer, Nancy.
Do you know me / Nancy Farmer ; illustrated by Shelley Jackson.   p.   cm.
"First published in the United States of America by Orchard Books, 1993"—T.p. verso.
Summary: Although he is continually getting into trouble,
Tapiwa's uncle becomes her best friend when he comes from
Mozambique to live with her family in Harare, Zimbabwe.
ISBN 0-14-036946-5
[1. Uncles—Fiction. 2. Family life—Fiction. 3. Blacks—Zimbabwe—Fiction.
4. Zimbabwe—Fiction.] I. Jackson, Shelley, ill. II. Title.
PZ7.F23814Do   1994   [Fic]—dc20   94-15027   CIP   AC

Printed in the United States of America

TO TELEPHONE MTOKO

Long may he drive.

chapter one

WHEN Tapiwa came home from school, the police car was already in front of her house. She knew why it was there. Father, Mother, and her older brother, Tongai, were outside. She saw the man in the backseat rap on the window. Then he rattled the door handle so hard it almost came off. Father went over quickly and opened it.

Uncle Zeka stepped out. He was older than Father and much thinner. Father was dressed in a business suit because he had just come home from the bank. Uncle Zeka was dressed in baggy pants that had been mended so many times they looked like a road map. His shirt was a grain bag with holes cut out for his head and arms.

Uncle Zeka looked at his new family and smiled. It was such a big welcoming smile that Tapiwa knew she was going to like him. "Have you eaten, my brother?" said Father, politely.

"Yes, thank you," said Uncle Zeka just as politely. "But it is always nice to have more," he added.

Then Father thanked the policemen, and the family went inside. Tapiwa and Tongai sat quietly as Mother placed dish after dish of food on the table. Uncle Zeka explained, between mouthfuls, how he had left his village in Mozambique and traveled to Zimbabwe.

"The bandits came in the middle of the night," he said. "They had guns and they forced everyone outside. They took everything valuable, and when they were finished they set fire to the huts."

"How terrible!" cried Mother.

"You were lucky they didn't shoot you," Father said.

"Some people weren't lucky," said Uncle Zeka. "After the bandits left, I searched the ashes of my hut. I had a bag of gold buried under the floor."

"Gold?" Mother said.

"Yes. Every year after the rains, I sifted the river sand. I found little pieces of gold like rice grains. A few times I found bigger ones like mealie kernels or lucky beans. I had enough to make someone a bracelet." Uncle Zeka held out his wrinkled palm to show how much he had had.

"You didn't find the bag, did you?" said Father.

"The ashes were very confusing, and I was afraid the bandits would come back. I decided the only thing I could do was come to you."

"Of course," Father said.

"I walked until I crossed the border. Then I walked

some more until the police found me. After that, I got to travel in a car all the way to Harare."

Uncle Zeka was excited about the car because it was the first one he had ever been in. He described how the wind blew in his face and how things flew past the window. He had to close his eyes every time the car turned a corner.

From the way Uncle Zeka talked, it sounded like nothing much had happened before the car ride. But Tapiwa knew he had walked through the bush for two weeks. Every day he had had to hunt for water and food without so much as a pocketknife. There were lions, leopards, elephants, and hippopotamuses in the bush, as well as many kinds of poisonous snakes.

"Do you have a car?" said Uncle Zeka hopefully.

"It's very old," Father said. "The air-conditioning doesn't work."

Uncle Zeka sighed. "This is a wonderful place."

Tapiwa sat on the floor, just below the edge of the table. She wanted to watch her uncle, but Mother saw the top of her hair over the tablecloth. "Change out of your uniform, Tapiwa," she said. "Shame on you for sitting on the floor. You'll get dirty."

Tapiwa went to the bedroom and looked into the mirror. She didn't think dirt would show on her school uniform. It was as gray as the floor already.

All her classmates wore the same clothes, to show they were from Lobatse School. They had gray dresses, brown shoes, and brown hats. Their socks were gray with a brown stripe at the top. Every morning Tapiwa's teacher lined the students up to be sure they were all alike. Once Tapiwa

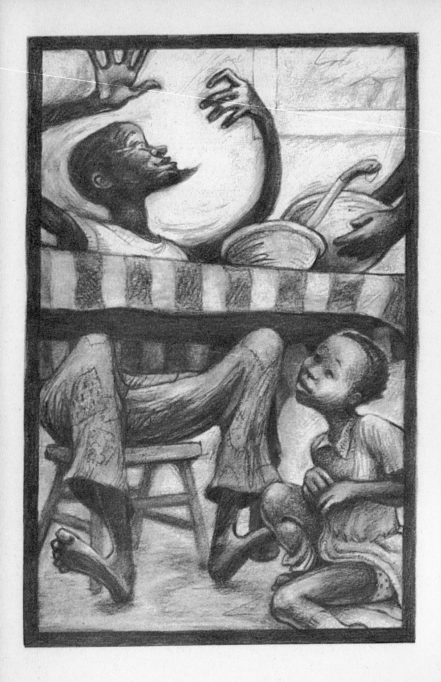

made a mistake and wore white socks. The other girls laughed at her, and the teacher sent her home to change. Tapiwa's face felt hot when she remembered that laughter.

She kicked off the heavy brown shoes and threw the gray socks under the bed. She changed into a bright blue dress and ran out to the garden. Tongai was showing Uncle Zeka the fruit trees.

"Guavas! Mangoes! Papayas!" exclaimed Uncle Zeka in delight.

"We have pineapples, too," said Tongai.

"Ah! So many!" Uncle Zeka clapped his hands. He admired the bananas by the fence and tried to lift one of the heavy bunches. Tongai showed him how to tell when the gooseberries were ripe. Uncle Zeka had never seen gooseberries before.

Tapiwa wanted to ask questions, but she knew it was rude to talk to elders unless they spoke to her first. She bit her tongue to keep the questions inside.

"Sugarcane!" cried Uncle Zeka. He borrowed Tongai's scout knife. In no time, he whacked off three pieces, whittled away the tough outer skin, and handed some to Tongai and Tapiwa. A trickle of sweet juice ran down into his beard as he ate.

"What kind of food did you have in Mozambique?" said Tapiwa shyly.

"The same kind you have in Zimbabwe," Uncle Zeka said. "Pumpkins, mealies, fish, and caterpillars."

"*Caterpillars?*" said Tapiwa.

"Quiet," Tongai hissed.

"We mustn't make him feel different," he said later when they were alone.

"I know people eat caterpillars," said Tapiwa. "I've just never seen anyone do it."

"Well, be careful. Father says it's going to be hard for Uncle Zeka to get used to things. He doesn't know how to use a telephone or change a light bulb. He can't read or write. He's just as smart as Father, but he never went to school."

Tapiwa hung her head and promised to remember her manners.

"Here comes the garbage truck," whispered one of the girls in Tapiwa's class at school. The others looked slyly at Tapiwa. They stood up straight as the teacher inspected the line. All the Lobatse girls waited eagerly at the school gate. When the clock struck three, the teacher would allow them to go.

Tapiwa gazed into the distance, pretending not to hear, but she was painfully aware of Father's car. It chugged and rattled between a long line of Rolls-Royces, Mercedes-Benzes, and other large and important cars. A few students were even picked up by chauffeurs.

"Bang!" went the exhaust pipe on Father's car as he brought it to a halt. The Lobatse girls nudged one another in delight.

Tapiwa often wished she could go to an ordinary school. Once she had. The headmaster there told Father she was his brightest student. Father was so pleased he borrowed money and moved her to the most expensive girls' school in the whole country.

It didn't take her new classmates long to find out Father was only a bank teller. It didn't please them when Tapiwa turned out to be the brightest student at Lobatse, too.

Tapiwa sighed—inside, where it wouldn't show. She saw Father wave happily at her, while the other parents sat quietly in their cars.

The bell rang, and the teacher stepped back from the gate. The orderly line of girls broke up into clusters of friends. They chatted and laughed as they left the playground. In the middle, Tapiwa walked alone. She had learned one very important lesson at Lobatse School: stay invisible.

Don't ask questions.

Don't complain.

Don't draw anyone's attention.

It was a lonely lesson, but it saved her a lot of heartache. Tapiwa pulled open the car door, wincing at the grating noise it made. "How was school?" said Father, with a big smile on his face. He asked the same question every day.

"It was fine," said Tapiwa. She gave the same answer every day.

And then they drove home. Tapiwa used the lesson she had learned at Lobatse on Uncle Zeka. She followed him around, but she didn't ask questions. She sat quietly at a distance while he dug a vegetable garden in the backyard. Day after day, she was always just around a corner or in the deep shade of a tree. When she did this, she became invisible to Father, Mother, and Tongai, but Uncle Zeka was different.

"I see my shadow," he called as he hammered a chicken coop together. "My shadow follows me everywhere."

Tapiwa smiled and looked down.

"Now I look sharp," said Uncle Zeka, lifting his feet high as he practiced with the new sandals Father had bought him. "Soon I will be as well dressed as you."

"I'm only wearing a school uniform," said Tapiwa, surprised out of her silence. She thought her uniform was ugly.

Uncle Zeka dumped wood shavings into the coop and stood back to admire it. "Do you know what the people wore in my village?"

"No," said Tapiwa.

"Parachutes! The Mozambique army used to drop soldiers from airplanes to fight the bandits. They had fine-looking parachutes—brown with green spots. After the battles, we harvested them from the bushes."

Tapiwa imagined the sky blooming with brown-and-green parachutes. What a magical way to get your clothes! She looked up to see Uncle Zeka grinning at her, and this time she didn't look away.

chapter two

ONE night, when the air was still and thunder rumbled in the distance, Uncle Zeka invited Tapiwa to hunt termites with him. She knew all about hunting termites, of course, but she had never done it after dark.

Father said it was old-fashioned to believe in ghosts and witches. Many people disagreed with him. Even Tapiwa's teacher had seen a witch riding on a hyena. The *muroyi* rode up to a man's house, the teacher told the horrified girls. She called his name and forced him to open the door. Then she sent her evil ghosts in to make him sick.

Everyone knew witches came out after dark. They were followed by owls that sat on trees and wished bad luck on people. Most of all, witches liked to steal children. They boiled them in pots to make a magic potion called *muti*.

Tapiwa remembered this when Uncle Zeka invited her on a nighttime termite hunt, but she wanted him to like her. She looked nervously at the dark window. After all, she thought, Uncle Zeka walked for two weeks through the bush without even a pocketknife. He must know how to stay out of danger.

"All right," she said.

Uncle Zeka found a large plastic bag in the pantry. Tapiwa followed him closely as he strode along the road to the edge of a *vlei*, a marshy wasteland. They stopped under a streetlamp and waited. Here and there, she saw termites boil out of the ground. Most of them were small and wingless, but among them were sleek, fat insects with wings. The fat ones were supposed to fly away and start new nests, but they didn't want to. The little termites ran around and bit them to make them go.

Soon the air was full of clumsy fluttering bodies from hundreds of nests on the *vlei*. Thousands gathered at the light, and Uncle Zeka and Tapiwa scooped them into the bag. Now and then they ate one. The termites tasted slightly sour and nutty. All around, frogs, toads, and lizards gathered to eat. Some of the toads were so full of food they couldn't hop.

Under other lights, people stood and caught termites, but Tapiwa didn't see anyone else with a large bag. She didn't know what Uncle Zeka was going to do with so much food, but maybe he planned to eat like the toads. She smiled at the thought.

"Look at that owl," said Uncle Zeka. Out over the dark *vlei*, a large pale shape swooped and turned. Tapiwa shrank

into a ball and covered the top of her head with her hands. The eagle owl veered across the road and carried off a lizard. Uncle Zeka threw a stone at the owl. It hooted with surprise and dropped the lizard. The bird flapped off until Tapiwa couldn't see it anymore.

"W-wasn't that d-dangerous?" she said from between clenched teeth.

"Ha! There's one witch who won't be making *muti* tonight," said Uncle Zeka with satisfaction. He explained that owls carried messages to witches, to tell them where children were to be found. "It's a good thing I'm here," he said. "When we get home, I'll give you my anti-witch medicine. Rub it on your skin. That old *muroyi* will never find you."

Tapiwa jumped at every sound on the way home. She wanted to run, but Uncle Zeka couldn't move quickly with such a heavy bag. Now and then he stopped to rest. When they got home, he gave her a little bottle of evil-smelling oil. She rubbed it all over her skin. Next morning Mother made her take a shower, but that night Tapiwa slept soundly.

Uncle Zeka rolled three rocks together in the front yard and started a fire between them. He hammered out a large tin can into a flat sheet. Then he roasted and dried the termites so they would keep.

"He ruined my flower bed," Mother cried later. "There's a burned place right in the middle of it."

"He didn't know it was special. He has never raised flowers," said Father.

A few days later Mother screamed when she took the

lid off a pot in the kitchen. Inside, dozens of fat, hairy caterpillars bobbed up and down in a kind of soup. They smelled disgusting. Mother took a deep breath and slammed the lid back on the pot. "We mustn't criticize Uncle Zeka," she told Tapiwa. "The people where he lived were so poor they didn't even have chickens. Tsetse flies and disease killed everything. They had to eat whatever they could find. I wish, though," she said half to herself, "that he would simply eat what I cook and not try to help out."

That night Uncle Zeka served his caterpillar stew, but no one wanted it. "I'm sorry," said Father. "We aren't used to this kind of food."

"You're missing a good thing," said Uncle Zeka, helping himself to a large bowlful.

In the night, he got very sick. Father had to take him to the emergency room at the hospital. The next day Uncle Zeka stayed in bed, looking gray and weak.

"I can't understand it," he told Tapiwa when she brought him tea. "They looked like the caterpillars I used to eat in Mozambique. Of course, those lived on pumpkin leaves," he said thoughtfully, "and these were on the death-apple tree."

"Oh, Uncle Zeka," Tapiwa cried. "They were full of poison. You might have died! Why don't you eat what Mother cooks?"

"I want to help out," he replied. "If only I had my bag of gold."

"Father doesn't expect you to buy things," said Tapiwa, but Uncle Zeka sighed.

"That gold was nice," he said. "You know, when a

farmer has many cows, he can still call each of them by name."

Tapiwa nodded. Everyone she knew liked to own cattle. Even Father, who worked in a bank, had a small field outside Harare. He had three cows, and on weekends he went out there to admire them.

"A farmer hates to sell a cow even when he doesn't have enough food," Uncle Zeka explained. "Cows tell how important he is. They are almost like family. Well, my gold pieces were my cows."

Then Tapiwa understood. Tsetse flies and disease killed off all the animals in Uncle Zeka's village. He couldn't own cattle. He had the gold pieces instead, and now they were all gone. She felt very sad for him.

"But I'm being silly," said Uncle Zeka with a smile. "I have a nice family now. What do I need with gold?"

It was Saturday, and Tapiwa didn't have to go to school. She lay in bed and smiled up at the ceiling. It wasn't—exactly—that she hated school. She liked to learn new things, but she didn't have any friends. Going to Lobatse, she thought, was like being locked up in the vault at Father's bank.

Father had shown her the vault not long ago. "This is where the money is kept," he said, waving at the boxes stacked against the walls. He closed the thick iron door and turned a wheel to move the heavy bolts of the lock. "Not even the army can get in now," he said proudly. "This is the safest bank in Africa."

Tapiwa had not felt safe at all. When the door closed, the friendly voices from outside disappeared. The air became dead, and the stale odor of money made her frantic to get out. She didn't breathe deeply until Father opened the vault again.

Five days a week Tapiwa went through the gate of Lobatse School. It felt like an iron door had closed behind her, but no one let her out again. Father had borrowed money from Aunt Rudo to pay her fees. The longer Tapiwa went to Lobatse, the more money Father borrowed and the harder it was to complain. She was trapped as surely as if the lock had rusted shut.

Aunt Rudo was Mother's sister. She had married the Minister for Progress, who was enormously rich. He had his suits made in England and his shoes made in France. He drove an expensive German car.

Mother was very happy when Aunt Rudo loaned Father the money. She didn't know how miserable Tapiwa was. The other girls talked about their clothes and horses and televisions. They looked at Tapiwa's uniform and knew it wasn't bought in a store. Mother had made it. They laughed because their mothers didn't have to sew.

But on Saturday, Tapiwa didn't have to feel ashamed. She could wear any old clothes and run through the garden with bare feet. She heard Uncle Zeka's voice, so she dressed quickly and went to find him.

He was mopping up a big bowl of cornmeal mush, or *sadza*, in the kitchen. "Hello, Tapiwa. Want to go on a mouse hunt?" he said.

"We're leaving after breakfast," said Tongai excitedly.

Tapiwa hurriedly ate and followed them to an empty lot between two houses.

"Mice like tall grass," Uncle Zeka said. "There are probably hundreds in there, fat as pigs, waiting for us to come and get them."

"Are we going to set traps?" said Tongai.

"Traps!" said Uncle Zeka. "We don't want just one or two. We're going to feed the whole family. Your father might even want to invite his boss over."

"I don't think Father's boss likes mice," said Tongai.

"Everybody likes them," Uncle Zeka said. "Now the best way to collect a lot of mice *is to set fire to the field*."

"We can't do that," Tongai exclaimed.

"We're too close to houses," said Tapiwa.

"Nonsense," said Uncle Zeka. "Grass burns so fast it will be out before you know it. Now you stand here," he said, and gave Tapiwa a large stick. "And you stand there." He gave Tongai another one.

"What are we supposed to do?" Tapiwa asked.

"I'll start the fire at the other end, and when the mice run out, you hit them."

"I don't want to do that! I don't like to kill things!" cried Tapiwa.

"Please stop!" Tongai said, but Uncle Zeka was already at the opposite end of the field.

He struck matches and walked along, setting a blaze. The fire shot up with a fierce crackling sound. The flames were red, and the wind drove them toward Tapiwa and Tongai. Black smoke poured into the air.

Above the sound of the fire came the squeaks of mice. They poured out of the grass and ran straight for the children. Tongai stood hypnotized, and Tapiwa dropped her stick. The mice ran between their feet and around their legs. Then the mice disappeared into the gardens all around.

A fire engine clanged its bell as it came around a corner. Men jumped off and began to beat out the fire with heavy sheets of rubber. Others ran to find water.

"You didn't catch anything," said Uncle Zeka in a disappointed voice.

"We've got to go," said Tongai, pulling at his uncle's sleeve, but it was already too late. The owners of the houses came out and grabbed Uncle Zeka. They pulled him one way and another and shouted at him. Tongai ran for help.

"You can't set fires in the city," said Father at dinner that night.

"I was only trying to help," Uncle Zeka said.

"I know," said Father. "Your problem is, you don't like to sit idle all day. We'll have to find you a job."

"That's an excellent idea," said Uncle Zeka, cheering up. "I can be a cook."

Mother choked on her *sadza* and had to drink a glass of water to calm down.

chapter three

THE car sped along the road past groves of *msasa* trees and tall, rustling fields of mealies. Now and then it passed farms of black-and-white cows. Tapiwa eagerly searched for the hills that surround Lake MacIlwaine. She was almost never taken on picnics.

Father and Mother had grown up in the country, and they didn't think picnics were much fun. They liked to go to restaurants, where the food was hot and didn't have ants in it. Tapiwa had grown up in the city. She thought it was exciting to sit on the ground and eat with her fingers.

She turned and looked out the back window. Aunt Rudo's elegant black car followed behind. She was so rich she didn't even have to drive. She sat in the back, and a chauffeur did the work.

Mother always invited her sister whenever they went

anywhere interesting. If Aunt Rudo wasn't invited, she got angry and hinted that she might not pay Tapiwa's school fees.

"I think you're going to like this job," said Father to Uncle Zeka. "Are you sure you know how to swim?"

Uncle Zeka pulled his head inside the window. He enjoyed feeling the wind in his face, but he couldn't hear very well outside. "Oh, yes," he said.

"You'll have to clear weeds from the lake so boats can get through. Have you ever been in a boat?" asked Father.

"Oh, yes," said Uncle Zeka.

"You mustn't go into the water if you can avoid it," Father said. "I just want to be sure you can swim in case there's an accident. Lake MacIlwaine is full of crocodiles. That's why you're being paid so well."

Uncle Zeka didn't say anything. After a moment, he put his head out the window again.

"I wish he wouldn't do that," Mother said from the backseat. "It's so dangerous."

"He'll get tired of it after a while and stop," said Father.

But Uncle Zeka didn't get tired. He stuck his arm out and tore off leaves as the car passed. Tapiwa thought that looked like fun, but she knew she would be punished for doing the same thing. Uncle Zeka was older than Father. No one wanted to criticize him, even when he was doing something dangerous.

They turned off the main road and went through a pass in the hills. Tapiwa could see blue water shining between gray-green trees. There were neat lawns for picnics, and a restaurant. Along the shore were little boats for fishermen.

Father drove to a dock where several men were waiting. Aunt Rudo's car stopped at the restaurant so she could have a snack while Father introduced Uncle Zeka to his new boss.

Tapiwa watched her uncle get in to a boat with three other men. They had long hooks for pulling up weeds. The three men laughed and talked as they started the motor. Uncle Zeka sat in the bottom with his hands holding on to the side. They moved off over the water, growing smaller and smaller. Tapiwa waved, but Uncle Zeka didn't seem to see her. He was still holding on to the side.

Then Father drove to a picnic spot. He got out the fishing rods, and Tongai took out the can full of worms he had dug up that morning. They went into the reeds to fish. Tapiwa wished she could go fishing, too. She wanted to walk barefoot in the mud and lie down on a grassy bank to watch the clouds.

But Mother called her to help with lunch. They waited while Aunt Rudo's chauffeur parked the long black car nearby. Aunt Rudo struggled out in high heels that sank into the grass.

"It's so hot," she said. "I don't see why people want to eat outdoors when they have comfortable houses to sit in. I think picnics are silly."

"I'm glad you came," said Mother quickly. "We wouldn't think of having a party without you. You've been so kind to us."

"Humph," said Aunt Rudo, but she looked pleased. "I hope you're making the most of your opportunity, Tapiwa.

Important people go to Lobatse School—even the daughter of the National Bank President."

Tapiwa remembered her. She had yanked a thread on Tapiwa's skirt so hard the whole hem came apart.

"You ought to make friends with the Nigerian Ambassador's daughter," Aunt Rudo went on. "I met her at the President's birthday party. Such a sweet child."

The Nigerian Ambassador's daughter had thrown Tapiwa's hat over the school fence. A car had gone over it before Tapiwa got it back.

"We're very grateful to you," said Mother, nudging Tapiwa.

"Thank you, Aunt Rudo," Tapiwa said, looking down. She quickly got to work on the picnic basket. She spread out a blanket and unpacked bottles of fruit juice and sandwiches. She flicked away ants when they got too close to the food. She became invisible.

"This whole trip is silly," Aunt Rudo complained. "Why couldn't you drop Zeka off and go straight home?"

"We want to stay until he finishes work. We aren't sure he'll keep this job," said Mother.

"I don't see why not. Anyone can clear out weeds. All it takes is a willingness to work." Aunt Rudo sat down with a sigh on the chairs the chauffeur unpacked from the car. She was so fat she needed two chairs to sit on. Tapiwa thought the little high heels must hurt, but they were certainly pretty. They were made of green silk, and so was Aunt Rudo's dress. Tapiwa thought she looked like a big caterpillar about to change its skin.

"Put that here! Don't bump it against the door! Oh, you clumsy man!" cried Aunt Rudo, as the chauffeur struggled to unfold a picnic table. He placed it in front of the two chairs and covered it with a red-and-white-checked cloth. Then he hauled an enormous basket from the car and began to unpack.

Tapiwa was thrilled. Aunt Rudo always had wonderful food, and she had a lot of it, too. The chauffeur brought out sausage rolls, potato salad, fried chicken, potato chips, cold ham, and candied sweet potatoes. For dessert, there were cream puffs, apple pie, and chocolate brownies. It made Mother's egg sandwiches look very dull.

"It was too hot to bring ice cream," Aunt Rudo apologized. When everything was ready, she told the chauffeur to go away. He got a small brown bag from the car and went off along the lake. He sat down on some grass and took out a small loaf of bread and a Coke. Tapiwa wondered if he minded not being able to eat Aunt Rudo's wonderful food.

Mother called Father and Tongai to lunch. Tapiwa felt very happy to be sitting under the trees with her family around her. She wished Uncle Zeka was with them, too. He had a lunch bag on the boat, but it only contained egg sandwiches and tea. When Aunt Rudo wasn't looking, Tapiwa wrapped a piece of chicken and a brownie in her napkin. She hid them in the bottom of Mother's picnic basket.

"Does anyone here know a man named Zeka?" said a voice nearby. Next to the cars stood a park ranger.

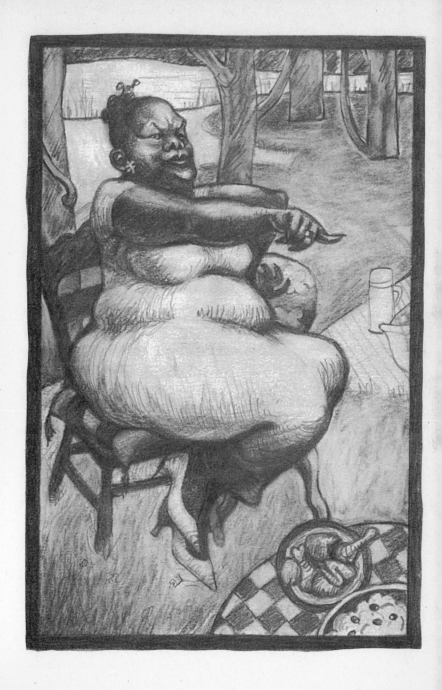

"What's happened? Has there been an accident?" Father asked.

"No, but we're having a little trouble with him," said the park ranger.

"Just what I expected," said Aunt Rudo. "He's completely useless. I suppose he wants to come back and get fed for nothing. Well, not with my food." She began packing things away.

Father jumped up and went with the ranger. Tongai started to follow, but Mother said, "Sit down. You'll only get in the way." She didn't notice Tapiwa, who was busily gathering up chicken bones to put in the trash.

Tapiwa dumped the bones into a can and walked away. No one paid any attention. She was worried about Uncle Zeka because he didn't understand things like motorboats. He might have done something dangerous. She followed Father to the dock, and there she saw the weed-pulling boat with Uncle Zeka inside. His hands were still gripping the side.

"He wouldn't do anything," explained the other workers. "He wouldn't take a hook or pull weeds. He wouldn't even get out of the way."

"I want him out of there," said the boss.

"Zeka," Father said. "It's all right. You're on land."

Uncle Zeka seemed to wake up. He looked around and saw Tapiwa. "Did you have a nice picnic?" he asked.

"Zeka, please get out of the boat," said Father.

Uncle Zeka opened his hands and moved his fingers as though they were very stiff. He stepped carefully onto the sand and took a few unsteady steps. "I don't think I did a good job," he said.

"Don't bring him back," said the boss.

"It's all right. Come and eat. You can tell me about it on the way," Father said. The farther they got from the water, the happier Uncle Zeka became. He told jokes about the men on the boat.

"You don't know how to swim, do you?" said Father.

"No," Uncle Zeka admitted. "When I was Tapiwa's age, a crocodile grabbed me by the leg and pulled me into a river. The villagers beat it with sticks and rescued me, but I have been afraid of water ever since." He pulled up his pants leg and showed a terrible scar that made Tapiwa feel faint.

"Why did you say you could swim?" said Father.

"I wanted the job," said Uncle Zeka.

When they got back, Aunt Rudo had packed up all her food. She sat in the shade of a tree, fanning herself. "I think it's a shame everyone was dragged out here for nothing," she said. "When I think of my nice cool house, I could cry. This heat is awful!"

"Why don't you go for a swim?" said Uncle Zeka.

Aunt Rudo sniffed and pulled herself up. She walked grandly to the car, leaving behind two rows of holes where her high heels sank into the earth. She closed the door and turned on the air conditioner.

Mother gave Uncle Zeka egg sandwiches and lemonade. Tapiwa unwrapped her napkin and gave him the chicken and brownie. Now he ate with gusto as he studied Aunt

Rudo's elegant black car. "Maybe I can be a chauffeur," he said.

"You have to read road signs," said Tapiwa before she could stop herself. Tongai rolled his eyes, and Mother frowned. Father cleared his throat. Tapiwa felt terrible. Why couldn't she learn to keep her mouth shut? They were trying to make Uncle Zeka feel welcome, and she had reminded him that he couldn't read.

But Uncle Zeka didn't mind at all. "Road signs!" he cried. "Anyone can *see* what to do. If the road turns left, you turn left. If it goes right, you go right. It's easy."

"What happens when you meet another car?" said Tongai.

"The important thing," said Uncle Zeka with a dreamy look in his eyes, "is to have the biggest car on the road. Then you can frighten everyone else into the bushes."

Father laughed. "I think you have learned a lot about driving already," he said.

chapter four

FATHER eased the car into the shade of a eucalyptus tree. It was even hotter than the day they had visited Lake MacIlwaine. Tapiwa could almost feel the cool blue of the swimming pool beyond the fence.

"Cheer up," said Father. "It won't be as bad as you think."

"It will be worse," said Uncle Zeka gloomily.

"No one expects you to work on a boat if you're afraid of water, but you should know how to swim." Father walked around the car, checking all the doors to be sure they were locked. Mother, Tapiwa, and Tongai stood in a row with rolled-up towels and swimsuits under their arms.

"Why should I learn to swim?" said Uncle Zeka. "I don't go into anything deeper than the bathtub."

"And he doesn't get out either," whispered Tongai to

Tapiwa. Mother frowned at them. Uncle Zeka had bathed in a stream all his life. He was so pleased with the tub he wouldn't get out of it for hours. He sang and talked to people through the door. Now and then he let out the cold water and replaced it with warm.

"Swimming is fun," Father said. "All of us enjoy it."

"I already know how to have fun," said Uncle Zeka, but he followed Father to the gate.

Sitting on a bench was a woman just as fat as Aunt Rudo. Her name was Bertha. Aunt Rudo always looked annoyed about something, but Bertha's face was cheerful. She took their money and gave them tickets to get in. "Are you going to have a lesson?" she asked.

"I haven't made up my mind," Uncle Zeka said.

"Yes," said Father, so Bertha collected another dollar for that.

"Do you ever go swimming?" said Uncle Zeka.

"Oh, no!" Bertha replied. "People always splash my hair, and I'm afraid someone will dive in on top of me. I don't even know how to swim."

"You're absolutely right," said Uncle Zeka. "It's important not to do things you hate."

"Come on," said Father, pulling him by the arm.

Tapiwa and Mother went into the changing room. In spite of all the times she had been in the pool, Tapiwa was still embarrassed to walk around in a swimsuit. Hers had bright purple and yellow flowers, but it didn't have a skirt. She wrapped her towel around her waist and didn't take it off until she was next to the water.

She dived in and swam along the bottom until she ran

out of air. Then she burst to the surface, scattering a spray of water. Tapiwa was an excellent swimmer. She had been taught by Cuthbert, the lifeguard. She saw Cuthbert on the grass at the end of the pool but was too shy to wave.

Cuthbert was lifting weights. He had a whole rack of them on a table under a tree. In the morning, before the pool opened, he swam sixty lengths just to wake up. During the day, he lifted weights or did exercises. He was wonderfully strong. Sometimes other men joined him, but no one could lift as many weights as Cuthbert.

Uncle Zeka came out of the changing room. Tapiwa suddenly felt sorry for him. He had on one of Father's bathing suits, but he was too skinny for it. He had a string tied around his waist to keep it on. He looked just as embarrassed as Tapiwa did in a bathing suit. Father came out, looking big and healthy. He waved at Cuthbert, who put down his weights and came over.

"I can lie in the little pool until I get used to the water," said Uncle Zeka. "I'll call you when I want to learn something."

"That's the baby pool," Cuthbert exclaimed. "You'll look funny in there."

"I like babies," said Uncle Zeka.

"Come on. You'll enjoy it once you're in." Cuthbert jumped into the pool and held out his arms. "I won't let you sink. Ask Tapiwa."

"He won't do anything frightening," said Tapiwa, but she wasn't sure about that. Uncle Zeka seemed frightened already. He stood at the edge, and she could see he was trying to think of excuses.

Suddenly, Cuthbert reached up and lifted him right off the side. He was so strong Uncle Zeka sailed up like a dry leaf and was in the water before he could even scream. Cuthbert planted him with his feet on the bottom and stepped back.

Then Uncle Zeka did yell. Everyone sunbathing around the pool sat up. Bertha jumped off her bench. Tapiwa covered her ears. The sun seemed to burn more brightly, turning everything into a sheet of brilliant light. Then the yelling stopped. The bright light seemed to go away, and Tapiwa saw Uncle Zeka standing again on the side of the pool.

"Maybe he ought to lie in the baby pool for a while," said Cuthbert.

"Should you give in to him like that?" Father asked. "How is he ever going to learn?"

"When someone is that afraid of water, it's better not to force him," Cuthbert said. "Bring him with you a few times. He'll relax."

Uncle Zeka went to the baby pool and lay down. The water just covered his body and his wrinkled feet stuck out. Several babies played around him while their mothers watched suspiciously from the side.

"It's a disgrace letting a grown man in here," said one.

"I think Cuthbert should throw him out," said another, and they glared at Uncle Zeka.

He didn't notice. He smiled at the babies, and they climbed over him as though he were a big rock. After a while, he got out and sat on the grass next to Bertha's bench.

A group of Lobatse girls came out of the changing room. They linked arms and walked past Tapiwa without a glance. She might have been a sparrow pecking crumbs off the cement. They chased some smaller girls away from a shady tree and threw themselves down on the grass. One girl switched on a radio at top volume, and Cuthbert told her to turn it off.

Tapiwa tried not to care, but their unfriendliness still hurt. She picked up her towel and joined Uncle Zeka and Bertha.

"Animals know how to swim without being taught," Uncle Zeka was explaining to Bertha. "That's because they're stupid. Humans are smart enough to know water is dangerous."

Bertha giggled and looked at him out of the corner of her eye.

"Do all animals know how to swim?" said Tapiwa.

"Everything! Mice, dogs, snakes, and elephants."

"Elephants?" said Tapiwa. She couldn't imagine anything that large floating in water.

"I was visiting some friends on Lake Cabora Bassa," Uncle Zeka told them. "That's a new lake on the Zambezi River. They built a dam, and the water filled up a whole valley." Bertha opened her lunch box and offered them sandwiches.

"When the lake filled up, many animals were trapped on the new islands it formed. They all swam to safety. Sometimes it took them days to make up their minds, but they did it. I saw trees sticking out of the water that were covered with snakes."

"Ooo," said Bertha.

"*Hundreds* of snakes," said Uncle Zeka, looking around as though he could see them right there on the grass. "They were wriggling and biting and snapping at one another."

"Ooo," said Bertha, shaking all over.

"What about the elephants?" Tapiwa asked.

"There were six of them on an island," said Uncle Zeka. "They stayed there until they had eaten all the food. Then they floated in a row down the lake with the tips of their trunks above the water."

"My goodness! I never heard of such a thing," Bertha said.

"There was a soldier who wanted to shoot them for ivory," Uncle Zeka went on. "He thought they would be easy to hunt. He took his gun and rowed out to where they were."

"What happened?" said Tapiwa breathlessly.

"The first elephant swung his trunk and broke the boat in two," Uncle Zeka said, and he helped himself to another of Bertha's sandwiches. "Boom! Everything went into the water—boat, man, and gun. Then the elephants continued floating down the lake with their trunks in the air. These are very good peanut butter sandwiches. Did you grind the peanuts yourself?"

Bertha lowered her eyelashes and looked pleased. Tapiwa had a sudden thought. "Uncle Zeka, you can't learn to swim from Cuthbert because you don't know him. You don't trust him."

"That's right," said Uncle Zeka. "How can anyone expect me to learn from a stranger?"

"But you know me," said Tapiwa.

Uncle Zeka stopped in midchew. He stared at a flowering vine on a wall. "Look! There's a honey guide," he cried, pointing at an olive green bird. "It will lead you to a beehive, if you promise to share the honey."

"Did you hear me?" said Tapiwa.

"Do you like honey?" Uncle Zeka said.

"I think it's a very good idea," said Bertha. "Tapiwa is an excellent swimmer. And she's a relative, so you can trust her."

Uncle Zeka looked unhappily from Bertha to Tapiwa. He slowly got up and brushed the crumbs from his chest. He went to the steps leading into the shallow end of the pool. Tapiwa held his hand and led him down. She went slowly. She was proud that he trusted her. When they got to the bottom, the water was up to Uncle Zeka's chest. Tapiwa led him slowly along the wall. He had one hand on the side and one on her shoulder. His face was frozen.

Suddenly, someone dived into the water, sending a wave splashing into his face. He struggled wildly and yelled. Father and Cuthbert ran to the side. "What happened? Are you all right?" Father cried. Uncle Zeka clutched the side of the pool.

"That's wonderful! You got into the water by yourself," said Cuthbert.

"Where's Tapiwa?" said Father. Uncle Zeka, still clutching the side, stepped off Tapiwa's stomach. She struggled to the surface, coughing and gasping. Cuthbert pulled her out and laid her on the grass. He pumped Tapiwa on the back to force the water out of her lungs. Uncle Zeka crept slowly along the wall and up the steps, but no one paid any attention to him.

Everyone gathered around Tapiwa. After a while, she was able to sit up and drink the tea Mother held to her lips.

"I know you were trying to help," said Cuthbert gently, "but teaching people to swim can be dangerous. You have to know what to do when someone panics." They all looked at Uncle Zeka, who was hunched under a tree, looking thoroughly miserable.

"He didn't mean to stand on me," said Tapiwa.

"I know what happened," said Bertha. "He was eating just before he went into the water. Everyone knows that's bad. He must have had a cramp."

"Yes, that's what it was," Tapiwa said.

"Of course! He didn't know you're supposed to wait half an hour after eating," said Mother.

Father brought Uncle Zeka back to the group. They all talked to him to show they weren't angry. "Tell us about the gold again," said Mother, so Uncle Zeka described how he found an especially fine piece shaped like a lucky bean. He was scrubbing a pot with ashes and sand when there it was, right in his hand!

As Tapiwa listened, she saw the rushing stream and the baobab tree on the bank. She heard the *mbira*, or rock rabbit, squeal with surprise when Uncle Zeka jumped up. The whole day was there, locked up in that little piece of gold.

Then he told Father, Mother, and Cuthbert about the

elephants in Lake Cabora Bassa. Everyone shuddered with horror about the trees full of snakes. "Did they finally swim to shore?" said Tapiwa.

"I think they swam after the elephants and bit them," said Uncle Zeka, "which proves my point: swimming is the most dangerous activity known to man *or* beast."

chapter five

BEHIND the house, a trail wound under jacaranda trees that were covered with flowers in the spring. The flowers fell to the ground until it was covered. Tapiwa loved the path then. It was like a purple rug with a purple sky overhead, unrolling past dust-berry bushes and into a thicket of reeds. The reeds had spiky leaves that cut her skin if she wasn't careful. She didn't like them, but Uncle Zeka did.

He didn't notice the flowers. Tapiwa pointed them out, and he asked what kind of fruit a jacaranda tree had. When he found out it didn't have any, he lost interest.

The path led to a stream with stepping-stones. Then it wound up until it came to a small store. Tapiwa and Uncle Zeka often walked there. Uncle Zeka always bought ciga-rettes—one at a time. Father gave him enough money to buy a whole pack, but he wasn't used to having so many at once. He got one in the morning and walked back to get another in the afternoon.

Sometimes he took Mother's frying pan to look for gold in the sand. He showed Tapiwa how to add water and shake the sand around. "Gold is very heavy, so it sinks to the bottom," he explained. Uncle Zeka looked for many hours, but all he found was a rusty penny someone had lost on the way to the store.

One morning, however, he sat down on a stone next to the stream. "Look at all these reeds," he said. "Don't they belong to anyone?"

"I don't think so," said Tapiwa.

Uncle Zeka took out the knife Father had given him and sharpened it on a stone.

"Don't you want to go to the store?" said Tapiwa.

"You go for me," said Uncle Zeka. He carefully counted out the price of one cigarette. Then he began cutting down reeds and stripping off the leaves. He started to sing, and Tapiwa knew it was no use waiting for him. She went on up the path to the store.

"You ought to be ashamed of yourself," said Mr. Magadza, the storekeeper.

"It's for Uncle Zeka," said Tapiwa in a small voice.

"Hah!" said Mr. Magadza, looking around at the men and women sitting on the front steps. "That's how they start. 'It's for my uncle,' they say. We know who's going to hide behind a tree and smoke."

"Children today have no shame," said a woman.

"Next she'll want to buy beer," a man said.

Tapiwa wanted to protest, but she couldn't speak. She turned and ran out of the store. Once she was hidden under the trees, she began to cry.

She felt humiliated, and the worst thing was she didn't have anything to bring Uncle Zeka. She hovered between the store and the stream until she calmed down. Then she went on and saw, to her amazement, that a large stand of reeds had been cleared.

"Hi!" called Uncle Zeka. "Where's my cigarette?"

Tapiwa burst into tears. He was up the hill in two bounds. In another minute, he found out what had happened. Without saying a word, he took her by the hand and marched up the path. He stopped on the way to sharpen his knife and stuck it into his belt.

"You! Get out of the way!" he yelled as he came out of the trees. The men and women scattered off the steps. Uncle Zeka marched into the store. "Do you know me?" he demanded of Mr. Magadza.

Tapiwa held her breath. That was how people started very bad quarrels. If the storekeeper said, "Yes, I know you," it meant he was ready for a fight.

But he said, "Calm down, *baba*. I didn't know the cigarette was for you."

"Do you think the children in my family have such bad habits? I will tell my brother what you think. I will tell my cousins." And Uncle Zeka went on to list all his relatives, including Aunt Rudo and her husband, the Minister for Progress. He hinted that Cuthbert and his weight-lifting friends might visit the store, even though Cuthbert was not a relative.

"Don't be angry," said Mr. Magadza when Uncle Zeka had run out of threats. "It's against the law for me to sell cigarettes to children. Let me make it up to you. I'll give you three free cigarettes."

"Six," said Uncle Zeka automatically. They bargained until the storekeeper had given him four cigarettes and two pieces of candy for Tapiwa. Then Uncle Zeka walked stiff-legged out the door, glaring at the men and women on either side.

Tapiwa followed him down to the stream. Her heart was too full to speak. No one had ever stood up for her like that.

"Why did you cut down the reeds?" Tapiwa asked when they reached the stepping-stones.

"I want to weave them into baskets," he explained.

"Can I help you?" she said shyly.

"Good idea! You can sell them at the supermarket while I go around the parking lot. When I make enough money, I'll buy a cow. I lost all my gold, but a cow is just as good. Then I can sell the milk and buy *another* cow. Soon I'll own a whole herd." Uncle Zeka's eyes turned dreamy as he thought about the herd he would own.

Tapiwa wasn't sure Mother would want her to sell baskets at the supermarket. She decided to worry about it later.

She and Uncle Zeka squelched through the mud along the stream to a pond thick with reeds. "So many!" he said approvingly. He found a strip of thrown-away tin and rinsed it off in the water.

Tapiwa watched as he bent the last few inches of metal

into an *L* shape. He sharpened the edge on a rock. She realized he was making a slasher, a tool for cutting weeds.

"I promised Bertha I would cut the grass at the swimming pool," Uncle Zeka said. "Ha!" He swung the slasher and chopped off a reed. He raised the tool again and froze. Tapiwa almost screamed when she saw what he was watching. It was a wild pig! The creature stared at them from the path.

It twirled its tail and wriggled its snout as it tried to pick up their scent. Then it bent down and drank deeply from the stream.

Uncle Zeka stood perfectly still, the slasher raised in the air. Tapiwa hardly dared to blink. It was a large boar with wicked-looking tusks, and it cocked one ear in their direction as it drank. When it was finished, it watched for a long moment before strolling up the path again. It disappeared into the reeds.

Uncle Zeka let out his breath in a long sigh. "Do you like pork?" he said.

"Yes," said Tapiwa.

He explained how to make a pig trap, drawing on the ground with a stick. "Of course, I promised to cut the grass around the swimming pool tomorrow. But next week will be soon enough," he said.

He shouldered the slasher and, watching carefully for the boar, led the way back home.

The following day Tapiwa had a wonderful idea. While Uncle Zeka was working at the pool, *she* would build the trap. She thought about asking Tongai for help, but then it wouldn't be her gift anymore. Uncle Zeka had stood up for her at the store. She wanted to give him the wild pig.

She put on her oldest clothes. She found a small spade and a bucket in the garage. She took Mother's bread knife from the kitchen.

Hole digging was hard work. The ground was criss-crossed with roots. She tried to saw through them with the bread knife, but it bent double. She pounded it straight again with a rock. The only place where the ground was soft was the path, so she worked there. Even then it wasn't easy.

Tapiwa wasn't afraid of hard work, though. She toiled and dug until the hole was up to her shoulders. By now she was down to the water line. Water seeped into the bottom. It made the dirt easier to dig, but the mud was as soft as quicksand.

Now the trap was well over her head. She hurled fistfuls of mud over the side, but most of it dripped straight back onto her hair. She realized she couldn't make the hole any deeper.

Tapiwa clawed her way out and lay resting on the ground. What a beautiful trap! It was the best thing she had ever made. There was only one question: would the pig be able to escape? Uncle Zeka told her to put sharpened stakes in the bottom, but she was too tired. She hoped the mud was sticky enough to hold the pig.

With the last of her strength, she cut reeds and covered the trap. She laid palm leaves and dirt over this. Then she stood back and studied her work.

It didn't look exactly like the rest of the path, but it

wasn't bad either. Humming happily to herself, Tapiwa went home. She almost made it to the garden hose before Mother caught her.

"Eeee!" Mother shrieked.

"Eeee!" shrieked Aunt Rudo from the porch swing.

"How could you get so dirty!" Mother cried. "There's mud in your hair and under your fingernails! What have you been doing?"

"Playing in the stream," said Tapiwa.

"It was probably Zeka's idea," Aunt Rudo said. "He's a bad influence. When Tapiwa is expelled from school, you'll remember what I said." She had a bowl of peanuts on her lap. They were disappearing into her mouth like bullets. Father and Aunt Rudo's husband, Progress Minister Soso, had come out on the porch.

Tapiwa never called Aunt Rudo's husband "uncle." He was too important. He never traveled anywhere without a pair of bodyguards who stood behind trees and made everyone nervous. Tapiwa could see them outside the front gate. They carried machine guns and wore dark glasses so no one could tell what they were thinking. At the moment, the bodyguards were amusing themselves by throwing a knife into a tree trunk.

"Children should not waste time playing in streams," Progress Minister Soso said, looking at Tapiwa. "They should study and work hard."

Tapiwa thought Progress Minister Soso always talked as though there were a crowd of people standing in front of him.

"You get in to the shower this instant," Mother said.

An hour later Tapiwa, clean and combed, came to the dinner table. Everyone was there except Uncle Zeka. She guessed he had stayed to eat with Cuthbert and Bertha.

"Being on time is a valuable habit for children to learn," said Progress Minister Soso. "It trains them to be useful citizens."

"She won't learn anything useful from Zeka," said Aunt Rudo. "By the way, where is he?"

"I don't know," said Father. "He went to the store for his afternoon cigarette. I don't know why he isn't back."

The room seemed to turn dark before Tapiwa. She clutched the edge of the table.

"Are you all right?" Mother asked.

"I know where he is," Tapiwa managed to say. She ran out the back door to the path. In the distance, she heard yelling.

"I'll get a flashlight," said Father from behind her. Together, they went toward the stream. The yells became louder.

"It's all right. We're coming," Father called. The pig trap was broken in, making a black hole in the middle of the path. Tapiwa could see the top of Uncle Zeka's head. The problem became clear when they tried to pull him out. Water had seeped into the hole, turning the bottom into a waist-high, sticky bowl of mud.

Father pulled and pulled until suddenly Uncle Zeka came out with a loud sucking sound. He clawed his way over the edge, splattering mud over Father's suit.

They helped him back to the house. Father washed him off with the garden hose, and Mother brought tea.

"That's a pretty good trap," said Uncle Zeka. "You forgot the sharpened stakes, though."

Tapiwa felt sick.

"You mean that was *your* doing?" Father shouted at Tapiwa.

"Oh, I taught her how," said Uncle Zeka.

"Now you see what kind of lessons he gives her," Aunt Rudo said. "She'll wind up in reform school."

"At least have the sense not to put a trap on a public path," said Father.

"You might have caught Aunt Rudo," Mother cried.

"The hole was too small," said Father before he could stop himself.

"Yes," said Uncle Zeka, sipping his tea. "It could only have caught something little. Like a pig."

chapter six

U NCLE Zeka sat down by the stream most of the day. "This is my office," he explained. "Those are my workers"—he pointed at the reeds—"and I am the boss." He cut down reeds, split them into long strips, and soaked them in the pond. When they were soft, he wove them into baskets.

The path ran through the center of the office, so he could talk to people when they passed by on their way to the store. He sat on a rock, and his fingers moved so fast that watching him made Tapiwa dizzy. His fingers seemed to know how to make baskets all by themselves. Uncle Zeka told stories, laughed, and sang, but his fingers worked at the same speed no matter what he did. He boiled tree bark to make a black dye. He used black reeds to make a pattern in the baskets.

Tapiwa and Tongai tried to copy him. The air was hot and stuffy. *Mopane* flies hovered in front of their faces and crept up to the corners of their eyes to drink. Tongai quickly lost interest, but Tapiwa worked doggedly on. At the end of the day, she had only one basket. It was lopsided, and one handle was larger than the other.

"That's very good!" said Uncle Zeka. "I hope you'll give it to me. I need something to carry bark in."

Then Tapiwa no longer minded the heat and flies. She thought there was nothing nicer than sitting in Uncle Zeka's office.

His baskets came in all sizes. Some were for shopping and others to carry laundry. Some were meant for dog beds and others to take chickens to market. When Tapiwa went down to the stream after school, there were always more, and the office kept getting larger.

On Sunday, Uncle Zeka loaded all his baskets up and went to the supermarket. It was the only place open on Sunday. He knew everyone would be there.

"Wear your oldest clothes," he told Tapiwa. "Don't wear shoes. You must look poor so people will feel sorry for you." He rubbed mud in her hair and on her face.

Tapiwa wore sandals to the supermarket because her feet were tender, but she took them off once they got there. The cement was so hot she could hardly stand it.

"Look at them," Uncle Zeka said, waving his arm at the cars and people. "They've just come from church, where the minister has told them to be kind to poor people. And here we are!" He strode on. Tapiwa hopped from shady spot to shady spot.

The people did not seem to remember what the minister had said. They looked at Uncle Zeka and Tapiwa with suspicion. "Get away from my car!" a woman said. "I don't want you stealing the headlights."

"I don't need a basket," said another. "I have a nice leather purse."

Tapiwa's face burned with embarrassment, but Uncle Zeka was not bothered. "People always act like this when you're after their money. Oh!" he said, stopping before a woman in an expensive, flowered dress. "Is that your dog in the car?"

"Yes," said the woman.

A flat-faced little dog with pop eyes pressed its nose against the window and snarled at Uncle Zeka. "What a nice pet," he said. "It must win prizes."

"Why, yes, it does," said the woman in a more friendly voice.

"I knew it!" cried Uncle Zeka. "The minute I saw it I said, 'That is the boss of all the dogs. That is the prizewinner.'" He tapped the window, and the animal threw itself against the glass in an effort to bite.

"It's a purebred Pekinese," said the woman, smiling. "There are only a few in the country."

"Does it have a bed?" Uncle Zeka asked.

"Why, no."

"You don't want it lying on the *floor*," he cried. "The red dirt around here is terrible. Once it sinks in, it never washes out. You might as well shave a dog and start over."

The woman looked upset. "What an awful idea! I never thought of that. Let me see your dog beds."

Tapiwa carried a pole across her shoulders on which hung baskets in various sizes. The woman selected one and paid for it.

"How about another?" said Uncle Zeka. "They make nice baby beds, too. Do you have a baby?"

The woman looked at him as though he were crazy. She put the bed into the trunk, while the Pekinese jumped hysterically around inside the car.

"Do you know what a dog like that is good for?" said Uncle Zeka after they had moved on.

"No," said Tapiwa.

"Leopard candy. There's nothing a leopard likes better than a little dog. It will climb right into a house to get one. It will walk through a room full of sleeping people to munch up a dog." He glared back at the Pekinese snarling against the window.

Slowly they worked their way around the parking lot. Tapiwa saw with horror a whole car full of Lobatse girls stop in front of a bakery. Four of her classmates piled out of the back. They were dressed in church clothes and wore plastic flowers in their hair. They carried stylish little purses. Uncle Zeka headed straight toward them, but Tapiwa hid behind a car.

Uncle Zeka waved his arms as he talked. The girls ignored him and inspected the bakery window, where cream pies sat on paper doilies. He looked around for Tapiwa to show off the baskets.

At that instant, the car behind which Tapiwa was hiding started its engine and drove off. The Lobatse girls turned away from the window and looked straight at her.

But they didn't see her! They gazed out at the parking lot and saw only a beggar girl loaded with baskets. She was of no more interest than the flies buzzing over the garbage cans. They shrugged and went in to the bakery.

Tapiwa jumped as a car honked at her. "There you are," called Uncle Zeka. "I thought a witch had carried you off." He hurried after a woman whose shopping bag was beginning to fall apart.

"Now it's your turn," he announced, after he had sold two more baskets.

"I'm afraid," Tapiwa said.

"It's a bad idea for you to sell things in the parking lot," agreed Uncle Zeka. "We don't want you turned into *muti*. But a witch won't kidnap you inside the store."

Tapiwa's head ached from the heat. She couldn't think straight. The store looked cool and inviting. Uncle Zeka led her to the door, straightened the baskets on her pole, and sat down against the wall.

"Aren't you going in?" she asked.

"I think you'll have better luck without me."

Tapiwa went through the door with her heart pounding. She couldn't imagine asking anyone to buy anything, but she didn't want to disappoint Uncle Zeka. She went to the frozen food shelf, scooped up some ice, and pressed it against her face. That made her feel better. She wandered up and down the aisles. The baskets bumped against the shelves, and once she knocked down a box of cereal.

A woman with a baby tied to her back was looking at boxes of powdered milk. The baby gazed at Tapiwa with a very sad face. She thought it must be too hot. It had on a knitted cap and sweater. It was tied to its mother with a big towel, over which was a shawl. There were beads of sweat on its face.

Tapiwa's hands were still cool from the ice, so she went near and pressed them against the baby's cheeks. It blinked and smiled.

"Hey! What are you doing!" yelled the mother. She turned around and grabbed Tapiwa.

"I was only playing with your baby!"

"You little snake! You were trying to steal from me!"

By now other people were attracted to the scene. The store owner ran up. "What's wrong? What are you doing with all those baskets?"

"I was going to sell them," answered Tapiwa miserably.

"This is *my* store," said the owner. "*I* sell baskets in here. You aren't allowed."

"I didn't know," Tapiwa sobbed.

"She was trying to steal from me," said the woman. "You'd better arrest her."

"No! No!" cried Tapiwa. She struggled to get away, but the woman held on tight. Then two things happened. The shawl around the baby came untied. It flopped open, and down fell a box of powdered milk, a bottle of skin cream, a pack of cigarettes, and a chocolate bar.

"Ah! Ah!" cried all the people around.

"I was going to arrest the wrong person," said the owner. The woman flung up her fists, the baby screamed, and the store owner yelled for help. Tapiwa ran for the door. She dropped all the baskets, but she was too frightened to pick them up.

She found Uncle Zeka asleep against the wall and woke him. "Please, please, let's go home," she said.

"Did you sell all the baskets?" he asked. Tapiwa explained what had happened.

Uncle Zeka stood up and stretched. "This heat is making me sleepy. *Maiwee!* They're noisy in there." There was a shout and the sound of breaking glass. Uncle Zeka ambled through the door. Tapiwa hovered at the end of the building, ready to run.

A police car pulled up. In a few moments, they dragged out the thief. She rolled her eyes and shouted shocking things at them. A policewoman carried the baby. Then Uncle Zeka came out with the baskets.

"Don't let me catch you in here again," the store owner yelled. His shirt was torn, some of his hair had been pulled out, and one of his eyes was swollen shut. "Don't get an innocent child to sell baskets for you either!" He shook his fist.

Uncle Zeka walked to the end of the building and collected Tapiwa. "More leopard candy," he said. They went to the gas station, where he bought cool drinks. Two little children watched them with wide eyes, and he gave them each a penny. Then they sat in the shade of a jacaranda tree and rested.

"I don't think I like selling," said Tapiwa.

"What I need is to make really special baskets," Uncle Zeka said. "Ones that no one has ever seen. Then selling will be easy. I'll be able to buy *two* cows and get rich twice as fast. Soon I'll have a cow for every gold piece I left in Mozambique. That thief broke over a dozen beer bottles in the supermarket." He chuckled and leaned back against the tree.

chapter seven

TAPIWA went to school the next day. She was terrified someone would recognize her as the beggar girl at the supermarket, but no one said a word. The four girls who had visited the bakery ignored her, as they always did. "I'm invisible," Tapiwa said to herself. "Or am I? *Maybe they can't see.*" She rested her chin on her hands as she considered this.

After school, she went down to the stream. In front of him, Uncle Zeka had a pile of very strange objects. "This is for carrying shoes," he said, lifting a foot-shaped basket with handles. "The buyers will have to get two, and I'll make twice as much money."

"People don't carry shoes. They wear them," said Tapiwa.

"Even better! They'll put these on their feet and never get muddy."

Tapiwa didn't say anything. She looked at the basket for carrying sugarcane, which was long and thin, and the one for watermelon, which was big and fat. She wanted to think up an idea, too, but it wasn't easy.

Suddenly there was a loud buzzing sound. Hundreds of bees swirled into the office and zoomed around Tapiwa's ears. She screamed and hid under a large laundry basket.

"It's all right. They won't sting you," said Uncle Zeka.

She didn't want to find out. She cowered until the buzzing died down. It didn't go away, though. It settled in one place. Curious, she lifted the edge of the basket and peeked out. A huge swarm of bees hung off a low branch not far away. She thought it was the most frightening thing she had ever seen. The bees crawled over one another and reminded her of boiling porridge. They seemed to be waiting for her.

"Uncle Zeka," she called. "If I crawl away with the basket over me, will the bees chase me?"

But Uncle Zeka didn't answer. His fingers were dancing through strips of reed. He was weaving a huge basket. It seemed to grow before Tapiwa's eyes.

She crept down the path, dragging her basket along like the shell of a tortoise. When she reached the stream, she cautiously came out of hiding. The swarm didn't move, although a few bees zipped around the office. Tapiwa measured the distance to the pond with her eyes.

When Uncle Zeka was finished, he made a lid. He put the big basket on the ground under the swarm.

"Can you shake the branch really hard so the bees will fall down?" he asked.

"No!" said Tapiwa.

"I'll put the lid on quick."

"No!" said Tapiwa.

Uncle Zeka sighed. "The trouble with city children is they don't learn the right things in school. Everyone knows swarming bees can't sting."

"No! No! No!" yelled Tapiwa. She watched in horror as Uncle Zeka banged the branch with his fist. The bees dropped off like ripe mangoes. They fell into the basket, and he slammed on the lid and weighted it down with rocks. Inside, the bees almost roared with rage. The ones outside glued themselves to Uncle Zeka's hands. Tapiwa thought she was going to be sick.

"Please run away!" she cried.

"Ha! These bees have met their master," Uncle Zeka said. "They will stay in there and make me honey."

Slowly, trembling, Tapiwa stole up to where her uncle was sitting. Bees climbed over his shirt and wriggled into his wiry hair. "Doesn't it hurt?" she said in a quavery voice.

"Not a bit. When bees leave a hive, they eat so much honey they get too fat to sting." And Tapiwa saw that while the insects were doing their best, they simply couldn't bend their bodies enough.

She was filled with admiration for her clever uncle. "How long are you going to keep them locked up?"

"A day or two, to let them get used to their new home. Then I'll make a hole." Uncle Zeka walked off toward home, and Tapiwa trotted behind. As they went, he flicked off bees. Now and then he jerked, and once he even said, "Ow!" So not all of them were too fat to sting.

The next afternoon Tapiwa was surprised to see a fire in the office. The center had been cleared out, and a heap of logs was burning. Uncle Zeka squatted at the side with Mr. Magadza, the owner of the store.

"I can get more wood when you need it," Mr. Magadza said. "Of course I'll have to charge you."

Uncle Zeka laughed. "I can *find* wood. Look at the railroad tracks. They only need enough to keep the rails apart. The bits sticking out at the side are wasted."

"It's a serious crime to damage a railroad. Anyhow, you have to be careful what kind of wood you use." Mr. Magadza poked the fire with a long stick.

"I know. Some trees are poisonous," said Uncle Zeka. "Hello, Tapiwa. Look what Mr. Magadza brought me."

Tapiwa saw, on a cloth mat, a huge pile of fish. It was covered with a net, and tied to the net by its leg was a big black crow. It clicked its beak at her.

"We're going to make lots of money," said Uncle Zeka. "Mr. Magadza's nephew works at Lake MacIlwaine. He'll catch the fish, I'll smoke them so they turn into *kapenta*, and Mr. Magadza will sell them."

"What's the crow for?" said Tapiwa.

"That's my special trick," Uncle Zeka said. "When the crows come to steal my fish, they'll see their relative guarding it. He'll tell them to stay away."

"Those are *my* fish," said Mr. Magadza.

"Of course," Uncle Zeka said.

"What's in that basket?" Mr. Magadza started toward it, but Tapiwa quickly ran in front.

"It's full of bees. Don't touch it!"

"A hive? It shouldn't be next to the path," Mr. Magadza said.

"I'll move it," said Uncle Zeka.

"I hope so. People get killed by swarms."

Uncle Zeka laughed. "You city people don't know anything about the bush. Swarming bees can't sting."

"I know that when they *stop* swarming, there's nothing wrong with them."

After Mr. Magadza left, Tapiwa watched Uncle Zeka knock the burning wood into coals. He scattered them into a square. Then Tapiwa helped him carry a low table from under the trees and set it over the coals. The top of the table was made of loosely woven sticks.

Uncle Zeka reached under the net while the crow tried to stab his hand with its beak. "This is a good watchdog," he said. Tapiwa worked from the other side, as far from the bird as she could get. They spread the fish over the table. Smoke curled up, and soon the air was filled with the smell of drying *kapenta*. It was a pleasant smell at first, but after a while Tapiwa got tired of it. She moved away from the smoke, but it seemed to follow her.

All afternoon she worked on a basket of her own, while Uncle Zeka stoked the fire and turned the fish. When he thought one was done, he replaced it with another. A huge flock of crows landed on the trees around the office. They cawed loudly and hopped from branch to branch. The crow on the ground cawed back. Tapiwa's head ached from all the noise, but Uncle Zeka was right. The crows didn't go near the net, and after a while they flew away.

Sometimes, the wind blew the smoke over the beehive. "Won't they get sick?" Tapiwa asked.

"Smoke is good for bees. It makes them sleepy," said Uncle Zeka. "They can take a nap and get ready to work."

Tapiwa thought the bees didn't sound sleepy. When the smoke blew over them, several bee voices rose louder than the others. Then the others answered until it sounded like a mob of people yelling at one another.

"What happens when they use up the honey in their stomachs?" she asked. "Won't they be thin enough to sting?"

"By the time I let them out, they'll be so hungry they'll go straight for the flowers. Then they'll come back and make fat honeycombs for me to sell. Bees are stupid," Uncle Zeka said.

That evening he loaded the smoked fish into bags and hauled them up to the store. Tapiwa dragged a sack behind her because it was too heavy to lift. Mr. Magadza and Uncle Zeka argued until Mr. Magadza agreed to provide more firewood and Uncle Zeka promised not to harvest the railroad track.

Tapiwa and Uncle Zeka walked down the path in the growing dark. Tapiwa stayed close, in case of witches. Uncle Zeka handed her finger-long sugar bananas from the bunch he got at the store. When they reached the office, the crow was fluttering at the end of its leash. A civet cat hissed at them before slinking off into the bushes. Uncle Zeka untied the bird and stuffed it into his sack. It bumped around inside and tried to spear him through the cloth. The fireflies drifted through the reeds, and tree frogs cheeped from the branches. Tapiwa thought she had never been so happy.

"When are you going to let the bees out?" she said next day. It was after school, and the office was full of fish and smoke. The crows were back. They seemed a little bolder. They sat on the lower branches, and one or two hopped up to the net. Uncle Zeka threw a rock at them.

"As soon as I build up the fire," he said. The crows watched with interest as smoke poured through the table and drifted over the hive. Uncle Zeka threw a bit of smoked fish at the pet crow, but it turned its back.

The *kapenta* didn't smell as good as it had yesterday. Perhaps it was the heat, but Tapiwa thought there was something unpleasant about the smoke. Then she saw a railroad tie covered with tar sticking out of the fire. "Uncle Zeka!" she cried.

"Only one," he said, noticing where she was looking. "It was a very little one."

"You'll go to jail!"

"I won't do it again. They don't burn at all well. I've been working on this fire all morning."

Tapiwa quickly pulled branches over the tie, but Uncle Zeka was far more interested in the hive. He took out a knife and began cutting a cookie-sized hole in the big basket. When he was finished, he stepped back. The piece of basket was still in the hole, but it trembled. Tapiwa could imagine the bees pushing on the other side. She watched, hypnotized, as the circle quivered, seesawed, and fell to the ground.

Instantly the bees poured out in a flood. The humming rose almost to a shriek. The crows exploded off the branches, too panic-stricken even to caw. But Tapiwa had no time to watch. She ran into the reeds, cutting herself on their sharp leaves. She didn't care. Gasping with terror, she tore through the marsh until she reached the pond and threw herself in. The bottom was slimy, and for an instant she thought her feet were stuck in the mud, but she managed to drag them free. She crouched in the ooze with her head under the water.

She held her breath as long as possible. Then she had to come up for air. A bee stung her on the top of her head. Tapiwa inched along, going deeper, until she needed air again. Another bee stung her.

She remembered something Uncle Zeka told her. She broke off a reed. It took her several minutes and she got stung several more times, but at last she had a breathing tube. She was able to stay down long enough for the bees to go away.

She felt dizzy and sick when she crept out of the pond— and where was Uncle Zeka? The office was empty. The evil-smelling smoke drifted over the empty hive. The bees were gone. Tapiwa suddenly remembered the crow. She found its leash going under the net. Very carefully, she moved aside fish until she found it. It was shivering, but it seemed unhurt. She pulled it out and smoothed its feathers. Then she untied its leg.

"Tapiwa!" cried Father, running into the office. "Are you all right?"

"I went into the water," she said. "Where's Uncle Zeka?"

For once, Father didn't seem happy about his brother. "He was afraid of the water, so he ran up the hill to the store. The bees followed him. They went into the store and stung everyone. Mr. Magadza had to use up all his insect spray to get rid of them. He's very angry. He called me as soon as he could."

Father sat by Tapiwa and hunted for bee stingers in her hair. Every time he found one, he said, *"Maiwee!"* and pulled it out. "The smoke smells strange," he remarked as he removed the twelfth and last stinger. "What's that in the fire? *A railroad tie?*"

"This has got to stop," he said to Mother that night. Uncle Zeka was in bed with a fever from all his bee stings. Tapiwa was in bed, too, but her door was open and she was listening. "First he got Tapiwa to build a pig trap," said Father. "Then he dressed her up as a beggar to sell baskets." Tapiwa cringed. She didn't know her parents even knew about that.

"He sent her to buy cigarettes," reminded Mother.

"Yes, and he stood on her stomach in the swimming pool. Today he almost killed her with bees. *And he took a railroad tie to use as firewood!* He could go to prison, *and Tapiwa was with him.*"

"I like Zeka," said Mother carefully.

"Of course. He's my brother, but we have to be sensible."

"Where can he go?" said Mother, staring out the window at the dark garden.

Father stared at the garden, too. "I have a plan," he said. But late in the night, Mother fell ill, so the plan was forgotten until later.

chapter eight

DOORS slammed; voices shouted. Tapiwa sat up in alarm. She heard the car start outside and Father yell at Uncle Zeka to open the gate. Tapiwa got up at once and went to the window.

It was still dark, although there was a faint glow in the east. The red taillights of the car sped off as Uncle Zeka and Tongai stood in the road and watched.

"What's wrong?" she called.

"Mother's sick," said Tongai. "Father had to take her to the hospital."

"Oh," said Tapiwa, sitting down on the bed. The news was so startling she couldn't think of anything else to say. It was like waking up and finding the house gone. Mother never got sick. She was always there, day after day, preparing meals, ironing, gardening.

"Your father says you must go to school," said Uncle Zeka. "He asked me to fix you breakfast."

"He said that?" said Tongai.

"Well, he told me to be sure you ate breakfast. That means the same thing."

Tongai quickly went into the kitchen and found a loaf of bread and a jar of peanut butter. "Don't worry, Uncle Zeka," he said. "We're big enough to look after ourselves."

At school, Tapiwa sat and stared out the window. The teacher called her several times, but she didn't hear. Father came for her and took her home at lunchtime. He looked tired, but happy.

"The doctor says we brought Mother in just in time. He operated this morning, and she's all right now."

"Operated?" said Tapiwa in a small voice.

"Oh, I forgot you didn't know. Mother's appendix was infected. It swelled up in the night. If she hadn't gone to the hospital, it would have burst."

Tapiwa imagined a balloon getting bigger and bigger. She shut her eyes and tried to think of something else.

"Of course, she has to stay in the hospital awhile," said Father. "The doctor says she's run-down. She has to rest at least two weeks."

"Can we see her?" said Tapiwa.

"I can. Unfortunately the hospital has strict rules about children. You and Tongai can only write notes."

Tapiwa felt tears come into her eyes. What good are notes? she thought. Mother didn't need pieces of paper. She would need people.

"Don't worry about being alone," said Father. "I've asked Aunt Rudo to take you."

"Uncle Zeka can look after me."

"That's a bad idea," Father said, with a funny look in his eyes. "That's a very bad idea."

So Tapiwa, Tongai, and Uncle Zeka packed suitcases. "Uncle Zeka, too?" whispered Tapiwa.

"Father's too busy to look after him," Tongai whispered back.

Secretly Tapiwa was pleased he was with them. Her heart sank at the thought of two whole weeks away from home.

Aunt Rudo's house had a high wall with broken glass at the top to keep out burglars. Above the glass was a live electric wire. The front gate was a sheet of black iron, with a hole in it so the gardener could see who was out there before he opened it. Inside was an enormous garden and a large swimming pool. The house was two stories high and had at least fifteen bedrooms. Marble stairs led up to the front door. All the windows had decorative ironwork on the outside, which Tapiwa thought was pretty until she realized it was also like the bars on a prison.

Aunt Rudo's furniture was rich and heavy, and the floors were covered with expensive carpets. Tapiwa didn't know which would be worse—tracking dirt on the rugs or walking on the floor between and dulling the mirrorlike polish. It was going to be a very long two weeks.

The maid showed her and Tongai to their bedrooms.

"You mustn't open the windows at night," she said. "That's when the burglar alarm is on." Tapiwa felt the bed, which was very hard, and looked hopefully for toys in the closet. There was nothing. There was a desk, where she could do her homework, and a copy of Progress Minister Soso's speeches to read if she got bored.

Tapiwa sighed and went out to find Tongai. "Where's Uncle Zeka?" she whispered. The long, dark, empty halls seemed to listen to her.

"She's so mean," said Tongai.

"Who?"

"Aunt Rudo. She hasn't even put Uncle Zeka in the house. He's in a *kaya* at the back."

Tapiwa could hardly believe it. She thought even Aunt Rudo couldn't be that unfeeling, but she was wrong. They found Uncle Zeka sitting in front of the servants' houses at the far end of the garden.

A wall in front of the *kayas* was covered with a massive honeysuckle vine. From the house, the garden seemed to end there, but *behind* the wall were the most miserable, run-down shacks Tapiwa had ever seen.

The roofs were made of rusty iron, the walls were blackened with smoke, the bathroom was a hole in the ground, and there was no shower at all. The gardener, maid, cook, chauffeur, and Uncle Zeka had to take baths in a tin bucket in the middle of a banana grove. There was only one faucet for everyone, and of course there was no electricity or heat.

"This is *awful*!" Tapiwa cried.

"Don't worry about it," said Uncle Zeka, accepting some tea from the chauffeur. It was boiled in an old tin can over a smoky fire. "You're the one I feel sorry for. I have lots of company, and I don't have to listen to Aunt Rudo and Progress Minister Soso."

The chauffeur laughed wickedly.

When Tapiwa looked more closely, she saw what Uncle Zeka meant. The *kayas* were poor but friendly. The gardener's small children played hide-and-seek among the banana trees, and their mother sang as she stirred a pot of porridge on a kerosene stove. There were no carpets to track dirt on and no dark hallways to watch her.

That night Tapiwa listened to laughter from beyond the green wall. There was no laughter in the front garden, where Progress Minister Soso's bodyguards lurked by the black iron gate. There was no laughter in the dark dining room of the big house. Aunt Rudo sat at one end of a long table and Progress Minister Soso sat at the other, with Tapiwa and Tongai in between. The cook, wearing white gloves, served them soup and salad and took away dirty plates. When they were finished with one course and wanted another, Aunt Rudo rang a silver bell by her plate.

Tapiwa and Tongai said nothing, but it didn't matter because Progress Minister Soso made up for it. He told them about taxes and property values. He told them why they must study hard and why they should not ask foolish questions.

"How's Mother?" asked Tapiwa when he paused for breath. Tongai stared at her in amazement. Even Tapiwa was surprised at her own daring: a few weeks before she wouldn't have dreamed of interrupting an elder.

"What was that?" said Progress Minister Soso.

"How's Mother?" Tapiwa insisted.

"You be quiet," said Aunt Rudo.

The Progress Minister waved for silence. "That is a natural question in a child," he said graciously. "Concern for parents is the foundation stone of our society. Your mother is fine, but that's only to be expected in the new hospital. Did you know," he went on, "that it cost two hundred fifty thousand dollars to build the new wing? And if you lined up the bricks end to end, they would reach all the way to Nairobi? They use ten thousand four hundred eighty cotton swabs every week and eight hundred gallons of rubbing alcohol. No other hospital in Africa can say that."

The Progress Minister's voice went on and on, as though he were addressing Parliament. Tapiwa could hardly hear the singing from the *kayas* in the distance.

The next afternoon Tapiwa saw Uncle Zeka outside her classroom window. He was carrying a large bag. "Look!" someone cried. "There's a strange man in the playground."

"He tried to sell us baskets at the supermarket," said one of the girls who had been at the bakery.

The teacher called, "Go away! We don't want anything."

Uncle Zeka stuck his head in the window anyway, and waved at Tapiwa. She stared at him, unable to think or move. She heard a murmur of laughter from the Lobatse girls. Someone whispered, "He had a beggar girl with him to sell baskets. Do you suppose—?"

And someone whispered back, "It was! It was her! I don't *believe* it!"

Tapiwa stood up and faced the teacher. "It's my uncle. He's come to take me home."

"Well, tell him he's too early. The bell doesn't ring for an hour," said the teacher. Tapiwa explained things to Uncle Zeka and sat down. Her legs felt weak, and her stomach hurt. She heard whispering all over the room.

Uncle Zeka sat under the window. From the sounds, he seemed to be eating peanuts. *Crack*, *crack* went the peanut shells. *Crunch*, *crunch* went Uncle Zeka's teeth. When he was finished, he sang a song about an elephant that got drunk from eating fermented *marula* fruit.

"I can't stand it!" the teacher exclaimed. "Tapiwa, you go home right now and take your noisy uncle with you!"

Everyone laughed as Tapiwa stood up. She was about to creep out in her usual invisible way when something stirred in her spirit. How dare they make fun of her family! How dare they laugh at Uncle Zeka! Put *them* in the bush without a pocketknife and see how long they lasted without being gobbled up by leopards.

She looked slowly around the room, staring coldly into the eyes of each girl. *Do you know me*, she said silently to the Lobatse girls. They stopped laughing and looked down. Even the teacher seemed uneasy. The room was totally silent as Tapiwa stalked out the door with her head held high.

"I tried to bring Tongai, but he has a soccer game after school. We have something important to do," Uncle Zeka announced as he shouldered the bag.

"What's in there?" Tapiwa asked, with a slight quaver in her voice.

"Oh, this and that. Do you want to see your mother?"
Tapiwa swallowed the lump in her throat and nodded. She
followed him to the road, where he waved down a pirate
taxi.

She had never been allowed to ride in a pirate taxi,
although she had often seen them. This one, like all the
others, was battered and rusty. The backseat was removed,
the back window broken out to make room for more arms
and legs.

The driver grinned at them and said, "Where to, *baba*?"
His front teeth were missing.

"Mufakose," said Uncle Zeka. "We have to do something before we visit the hospital," he explained to Tapiwa.
He and the driver haggled over the price before Uncle Zeka
tied the bag to the roof.

Uncle Zeka and Tapiwa crawled in with the other passengers. They flattened themselves against the side, but Tapiwa could hardly breathe. The woman next to her reeked
of cheap perfume. A small baby lay against the woman's
shoulder and whimpered.

The driver took off in a cloud of exhaust. He sang and
jerked back and forth to a dance tune. He slapped the car
door to keep time. Some of the passengers joined in, and
the car seemed to bounce along the road. Tapiwa felt slightly
hysterical, but her unhappy mood floated away with the
loud music. She amused herself by tickling the baby.

When someone wanted out, he banged on the ceiling,
but often the driver didn't hear him. The car went two or
three blocks too far, while the irritated passenger tried to
yell over the music.

The taxi finally reached old Mufakose at the edge of Harare. Then Tapiwa and Uncle Zeka walked down a narrow alley where half-starved dogs bristled and growled as they passed. At the end of the alley was a dark doorway. If she had been alone, Tapiwa would have run away. Even with Uncle Zeka, the door didn't look safe, but she gritted her teeth and went in. If it helped her see Mother, it was worth it.

Inside, things were even worse. Dried animals were nailed to the walls. Strings of strange withered fruits hung from the ceiling. Collections of bones were arranged on a table. In the corner—she almost screamed—sat an ancient man wearing a feathered hat. He watched her with glittering eyes.

"Have you spent the day well, *vababa*?" said Uncle Zeka, extrapolitely.

"I have done so, if you have done so," replied the old man, with equal politeness. "What can I do for you?"

Uncle Zeka explained about Mother's illness.

"I could do a better job if your brother would let me visit her," said the old man.

"He doesn't believe in traditional medicine," Uncle Zeka said, in the same way he would have said, "He's crazy." Both Uncle Zeka and the old man clicked their tongues over such foolishness.

"To know what's wrong with your sister-in-law, I need something she's touched," said the old man. Uncle Zeka opened the bag and took out Mother's comb. It gave Tapiwa a funny feeling to watch the old man turn the pretty red comb in his clawlike hands. She wanted to reach out

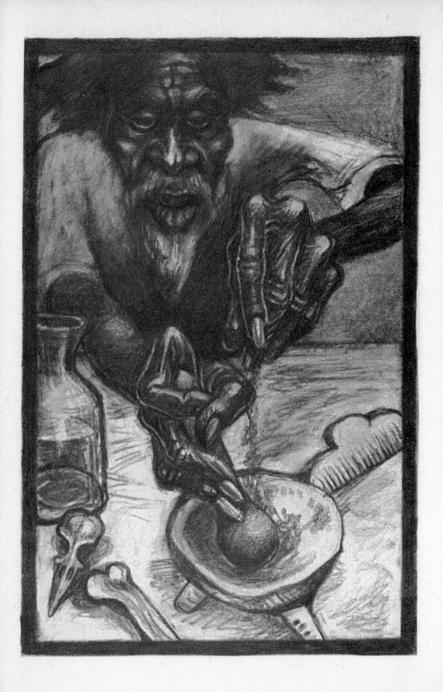

and snatch it back. "She's been bewitched," he said at last. "I'll try to protect her."

The old man ground up herbs and pieces of dried bark with a wooden mortar and pestle. He mixed the powder with oil. The oil smelled strange. It made Tapiwa think of dark forests and owls. She didn't want to know what it was. When the old man was finished, he put the medicine into a bottle and gave it to Uncle Zeka. "This isn't the best I can do, but it ought to work. Tell your sister-in-law to rub it over her body."

Uncle Zeka paid him. Tapiwa was upset to see how much money he had to give. She knew it was most of what he had earned making baskets. Now he wouldn't be able to buy a cow. He wouldn't have milk to sell to buy more cows until he had one for every gold piece he had left in Mozambique.

It wasn't until they reached the bright sunlight that Tapiwa breathed easily again. "Uncle Zeka," she said. "Are you sure that man wasn't . . . that he wasn't a *witch*?"

Uncle Zeka laughed heartily. "As if I would go to a witch! That man is a *nganga*, a healer. He's completely different from a witch. Don't go there by yourself, though," he added.

When they got to the hospital, Uncle Zeka didn't go in the front door. He went around to the fire escape behind a hedge.

"Are we allowed to use this?" whispered Tapiwa.

"Of course," he said. "This is a special entrance for children so they won't disturb the doctors." He climbed up rapidly to the second floor and went through a window. Tapiwa followed, her heart pounding.

The hall inside was empty, but doors opened onto large rooms. Uncle Zeka seemed to know exactly where he was going. He went to the third door on the right and looked in.

"Zeka?" said Mother from the bed. "*Tapiwa?* How did you get here?"

Tapiwa started to cry. She couldn't help it. She ran over and buried her head in the covers.

"Oh, my, Zeka, what have you done now?" Mother sighed. "Please don't cry, Tapiwa. I'm all right."

"It isn't visiting hours, is it?" said a woman in the next bed.

"I thought children weren't allowed," said an old woman with her leg in a cast.

"They aren't," said Mother wearily. She lay back on the pillow and rested her hand on Tapiwa's head.

"Look what I brought you," said Uncle Zeka, opening the bag. He removed ripe papayas, a chocolate cake, sausage rolls, a box of candy, grapes that Aunt Rudo had been guarding in her greenhouse, a cheese with a red, waxy cover, and several cans of sardines that Progress Minister Soso had gotten in South Africa.

Mother started to laugh. She laughed until the tears ran down her face. "Oh! Oh! That makes my stitches hurt! Oh! Rudo is going to turn *purple* with rage. You're wonderful, Zeka. You're the only one who thought about bringing me a present. But do you know what the best present of all is?"

"Tapiwa," said Uncle Zeka.

"Yes," Mother said. "You have no idea how lonely I get. Visitors are allowed only a half hour in the morning and evening. I'm sure I'd get better quickly if Tapiwa could stay with me."

"Do you want something to eat?" Tapiwa said.

"I wish I could have something, but the doctor put me on a special diet."

"There's nothing wrong with *my* stomach," said the old woman with the cast. So Uncle Zeka cut slices of papaya and cake, opened the candy and sardines, and passed around sausage rolls to the other people in the room. He and Tapiwa sat on the floor and joined in.

"This is like a party," said the woman in the next bed.

"I haven't had fish like this in years," said the old woman, wiping her greasy fingers on the sheets.

Mother laughed and talked. She had already begun to look better, but Uncle Zeka gave her the special medicine to be sure. "Rub it on your skin," he said. "It will protect you from spells."

"You listen to him," said the old woman. "If I had that kind of help, I'd be out of here tomorrow."

"What's going on!" came a voice from the door. Two nurses, a doctor, and some orderlies were crowded there. "I could hear you on the next floor!" cried the doctor. "Laughing! Singing! What do you think you're doing?"

"Having a party," said the old woman.

"I put everyone in here on a special diet!" the doctor shouted. "Look what you're feeding them—candy! cake! sausage rolls! You're poisoning my patients!"

"I am not," said Uncle Zeka.

"Don't you talk back to me! This is my hospital!"

"Oh, go away," the old woman said. "He gave us the best food we've had in years."

"Yes," said the woman in the next bed. "We haven't had so much fun since we got here."

The doctor signaled to the orderlies. They picked up Uncle Zeka and carried him out. A nurse grabbed Tapiwa by the arm and dragged her along.

"Here's what I think of hospital food!" shouted the old woman. She threw the sardine can at the doctor, and it splashed oil over his coat.

Tapiwa and Uncle Zeka weren't allowed to stop until they were on the street outside the hospital. "Don't try to come back, or we'll call the police!" yelled a nurse.

Uncle Zeka brushed off his coat and felt himself over for bruises. "I think your mother was glad to see you," he said.

Tapiwa smiled. "Yes, I think she was."

That night Aunt Rudo shouted and scolded about the missing food. She couldn't complain very long, since it was a gift to her sister, but she did send Tapiwa to bed early. Progress Minister Soso was out of town, and Aunt Rudo had no one to talk to and nothing to do. She settled herself in front of the television with a large bowl of ice cream.

Tapiwa climbed to the top of the bars covering her window and tried to look over the green wall. She was only able to see into the garage, but what she saw almost made her faint.

The garage doors were open, and Progress Minister Soso's Mercedes-Benz was parked halfway out. The chauffeur sat in the passenger seat with a bottle of beer. Next to him, behind the wheel, was Uncle Zeka.

chapter nine

"**D**on't take food out of the refrigerator," said Aunt Rudo. "The maid will give you lunch."

"All right." Tapiwa sighed.

"I don't want you digging in the garden. Oh, and stay away from the mangoes. I'm saving them for a party."

"Okay," Tapiwa said.

"I won't be back till dark, so you're on your own. Remember, tomorrow your mother is coming home from the hospital. You want me to give her a good report, don't you?"

"Of course," Tapiwa said.

"Good. Now where's my purse?"

The purse was easy to find. It was huge and made out of crocodile skin. Aunt Rudo said it was stylish, but Tapiwa thought it was creepy. The purse was loaded with perfumes and makeup and chocolate bars in case Aunt Rudo felt faint.

Her aunt fussed a while longer in front of the mirror. She was going to a meeting of the War on Hunger Ladies Club. The most important women belonged to it. Aunt Rudo was proud to be a member. They always met in the best restaurants. There were delicious buffets, and people could fill their plates up as often as they liked. Aunt Rudo looked forward to the meetings.

A car honked outside the iron gate, and the gardener went to look through the spy hole. A moment later a white Rolls-Royce drove in. "That's the National Bank President's wife," said Aunt Rudo. Tapiwa noticed that she never used the names of her friends. They were always somebody's wife, and the somebody was always important.

"It's too bad you can't go in your own car," she said.

"Well, I could hardly have a *drunk* chauffeur," snapped Aunt Rudo.

Tapiwa didn't say anything. She knew the chauffeur had not been fired for drinking. He had asked for a raise.

Aunt Rudo squeezed into the backseat of the Rolls-Royce, and it went out the gate. Tapiwa suddenly felt happier than she had for two weeks. Progress Minister Soso was out of town. Aunt Rudo would be gone until dark. The garden was full of sunlight. She didn't bother to visit the kitchen. The maid would be watching the refrigerator, and the pantry would be locked. Even the sugar was kept in a metal box with a padlock on it. Lunch, she knew, was going to be stale sandwiches with margarine on them. It didn't bother her. Tomorrow Mother was coming out of the hospital, and she was going home.

She went toward the *kayas*, but she stopped when she saw the big black Mercedes in the driveway. Uncle Zeka was polishing the mirrors.

"It's too bad the chauffeur isn't here," Tapiwa said. "He could have taken us for a drive."

"We don't need him," said Uncle Zeka, tossing the car keys up in the air and catching them.

"*Maiwee!* How did you get them?" Tapiwa cried.

"He gave them to me," said Uncle Zeka. "He said it was a good-bye gift to Aunt Rudo. I don't know why he wanted to give her anything."

Tapiwa swallowed hard, watching the car keys flash into the air and land again in her uncle's rough palm. "You don't know how to drive."

"Cars are like donkey carts," he said. "You pull the reins to get the cart to go right or left, and you rap the donkeys with a stick to make them go faster. It's just like the *accelerator*." He said the word *accelerator* slowly and proudly.

"You don't have a license."

"Beginners don't need them," said Uncle Zeka. "How else would they learn? They have to practice, and they can't do that in the garage."

Tapiwa knew there was something wrong with that idea, but she couldn't put it into words. Still, Uncle Zeka and the chauffeur had spent every evening in the car, so he must know about driving by now.

She watched him take out a bottle of oil and carefully go over all the moving parts of the car. "Cars like oil," he explained, rubbing it into the wheels. "It makes them go faster."

When he was finished, he wiped his hands on a rag and opened the door. "Want to go on a picnic?" he said.

Tapiwa hesitated. She wished Tongai were home so she could ask his advice, but he was at a Scout meeting. Father was at work. Progress Minister Soso was in South Africa. Aunt Rudo was at the War on Hunger Ladies Club meeting.

Uncle Zeka dusted the seat with the oily rag and turned on the car radio. Loud music poured into the garden.

"We don't have any food," said Tapiwa.

"*What?*" shouted Uncle Zeka over the music.

"*We don't have food!*"

"*We don't need it! Bertha is coming!*" he shouted. The music put everyone into a good mood. The gardener bobbed in time to it as he weeded. His children bounced around like mice. The maid clapped her hands at the window and smiled. Tapiwa got in to the car and fastened the seat belt. Uncle Zeka started the motor.

The car bounded forward and then stalled. "*Wrong gear!*" he shouted. He started again more slowly and crept out onto the street. Tapiwa was relieved to see it was deserted. Uncle Zeka turned off the radio. "We have to listen, to know when to change *gears*," he explained. He said *gears* as though it were a word in another language. He fiddled with the controls. Once again the car bounded forward, and he had to steer in and out of the jacaranda trees along the sidewalk until he got it right.

"The way to know when to change *gears*," said Uncle Zeka, "is when the car begins to cry."

"What do you mean?" said Tapiwa.

Uncle Zeka went faster until a piercing noise came from the motor. "There! The car is crying. It is saying, 'Give me another *gear*.'" He moved the controls, and the Mercedes jerked forward and stopped making the noise. "Another thing to watch for is back talk. Cars are like donkeys. If they don't want to pull the cart, they try to kick you."

He slowed down until the Mercedes began to shake. It rattled so hard Tapiwa had to clench her teeth. "Now it is saying, 'Please, master, give me a lower *gear*.'" Uncle Zeka worked the controls and the car stopped shaking.

"You see, it's easy." He drove along the tree-shaded streets, stopping now and then to adjust the mirrors or polish the windshield.

"I don't think you're supposed to drive down the middle of the road," Tapiwa said.

"That's the best way," explained Uncle Zeka. "You won't run into trees and so forth."

But just then a truck came at them from a side street. Uncle Zeka was so surprised he drove into a hawthorn hedge. Tapiwa heard the branches scrape the side, and one even popped into the window and slapped her in the face. The truck driver leaned out his window and shouted insults before he rolled on.

"Maybe you're right," Uncle Zeka said. "There are a lot of bad drivers around. We have to be careful." He drove up and down the back streets to practice before he turned onto a busy road. Once a policeman followed them on his motorcycle, but when he saw it was a government car, he drove away.

Uncle Zeka edged onto Second Avenue between a truck and a bus. Tapiwa closed her eyes. The car moved in a dizzy way, back and forth across the traffic. She heard the bus slam on its brakes and people shout, but the cries were left behind as they jerked forward. She found that keeping her eyes shut made her carsick.

"There's only one rule of driving," Uncle Zeka said, swinging in front of a pirate taxi with its horn blaring.

"What?" Tapiwa gasped. She felt really sick with all the weaving and wondered whether there was a paper bag in the car.

"Leave your accidents behind you," said Uncle Zeka. "This car can go very fast, but I want more room before I try it."

Tapiwa saw spots in front of her eyes, but just then they rolled onto the green lawn in front of the swimming pool and jolted to a stop. She crawled out and lay on the grass.

"What's wrong with Tapiwa?" said Cuthbert.

"Maybe she's getting the flu," Uncle Zeka said. "She was all right a few minutes ago."

Bertha got everyone Cokes, and they all sat on the grass. After a while, Tapiwa felt better. "I wish I didn't have to work," said Cuthbert. "That certainly is a nice car."

"I'll take you another day," Uncle Zeka promised.

The women who worked in the post office and the supermarket were sitting on the lawn with their lunches. "Soon they will see me being driven by a chauffeur in a Mercedes-Benz," joked Bertha. She smiled and waved at them.

Tapiwa was pleased to see Bertha had brought a heavy lunch basket. Uncle Zeka loaded it into the trunk. Then

Bertha got into the backseat, and he and Tapiwa got into the front.

"Now I'm the President's wife," said Bertha. "Chauffeur, drive me to the jewelry store. I'm fresh out of diamonds." She nodded grandly to the women on the lawn. The effect was only slightly spoiled when the Mercedes leaped from the grass and bounced onto the street.

"It's crying," said Tapiwa.

"I know," said Uncle Zeka, changing the *gear*.

Soon they were speeding along the farm roads at the edge of Harare. Uncle Zeka showed them how to save money when they went down hills. "You turn off the motor," he explained. "If the hill is really steep, you can go as fast as a racing car."

"Eeeeee!" shrieked Bertha as they got to the bottom and screeched around a corner.

They flashed along marshes and fields where cows looked up at them in surprise. Once they passed a huge field of sunflowers. The big blooms were turned toward the road as though they were watching, and the yellow was so bright it hurt Tapiwa's eyes. They rolled up hills where pink and white cosmos flowers batted at the windows.

"These are the Sengerera Hills," said Bertha. "There used to be gold mines around here."

"Gold mines?" Uncle Zeka said.

"Yes, people used to dig their own. The hills are full of old tunnels."

"I wonder if there is any gold left in them," Uncle Zeka said.

The sun glinted off the black hood of the car as it

climbed the hill. Uncle Zeka must have had it in the right *gear*, because it purred along with no more sound than a sewing machine. This is a wonderful car, thought Tapiwa. She could ride in it for days.

"Now I am going to save more money," said Uncle Zeka.

It was the steepest hill yet. Uncle Zeka switched off the motor, and the Mercedes began to go down. It went faster and faster. At the bottom was a bend in the road.

"Please put on the brakes," said Bertha.

"Ha! You are frightened," Uncle Zeka cried. "Don't worry. This is a strong car."

"But the motor isn't on!" Bertha wailed. "Stop! Stop! *Eeeeee!*" she screamed as the car reached the bend and missed the turn. It went bumping over the rocks, banging the bottom in a sickening way. Tapiwa grabbed the door handle, and then she screamed, too, as the mouth of an old mine loomed up.

The car plunged into the hole and came to a stop on a small tree partway down. Below, Tapiwa could see a gridwork of branches blocking the mouth of a deep black pit.

"Don't move," Bertha whispered. "I'm going to open the back door and try to get out. Then I'll help you." The front doors, Tapiwa saw, were stuck in the hole, but the back ones were still up in the air.

Slowly, carefully, Bertha opened the door. The car shivered, and a branch broke. Uncle Zeka turned on the headlights. The gridwork of branches was not far away, but beyond it the lights were lost in darkness. "They must have put that there to keep cattle from falling in," he remarked.

"It won't hold a car, though," said Bertha. "Now I'm going out." She edged through the door, freezing when the car trembled. When she was out, she sat on the open door to keep the car from slipping. "Climb up slowly, Tapiwa. I'll help you."

Tapiwa thought she couldn't move, her terror was so great, but Uncle Zeka smiled at her. He seemed so confident, some of her fear began to go away. She unsnapped the seat belt and began to creep over the seat. The car shifted, and she clung to it in a panic.

"Don't be frightened. I'll pull you up," said Bertha.

"And I'll push you," said Uncle Zeka. But just then the small tree snapped in two. Bertha was thrown backward as the car fell further to land on the cattle grid. The branches snapped and bulged.

Now all four doors were jammed into the hole. Tapiwa clung to the seat and looked up at Bertha's face in the sunlight. Uncle Zeka edged past her with a wrench. He bashed out the glass in the back window. "Now we can use this as a pirate taxi," he joked. He pried Tapiwa's fingers from the seat and eased her through the opening. Splinters of glass clung to the edge of the window. She cut herself and cried out.

"Slowly, slowly," said Uncle Zeka. Tapiwa inched a little farther. It seemed to take forever, but at last she hooked her fingers over the bumper and lifted her ankles past the jagged glass. She crouched on the trunk of the car. "Stand up," said Uncle Zeka.

"I might make the car fall."

"Hurry up. We want to get the picnic basket, too."

How can he think of lunch? Tapiwa thought desperately. Doesn't he understand the danger we're in?

"Take my hands," said Bertha. She was lying on her stomach by the hole, with her head and arms hanging down. Trembling, Tapiwa raised herself to a standing position. She lifted her arms. The big woman grasped her wrists and heaved her up. At the same instant, the cattle grid snapped. Bertha clutched Tapiwa and wailed. Together they watched the Mercedes plunge through the broken grid and rumble on down the shaft, with Uncle Zeka inside.

chapter ten

BERTHA rocked back and forth, sobbing, "Oh, that kind man! That good man! He's gone!" She squeezed Tapiwa so hard it hurt. Tapiwa was trembling with shock, but her mind was busy.

It doesn't do any good to fall apart, she thought. Uncle Zeka never did. No matter how much trouble he got into, he always got out again.

But falling down a bottomless pit? she thought, gasping as Bertha squeezed her again. Even Uncle Zeka couldn't fly.

Stop that, Tapiwa told herself. What would her uncle do now? *He wouldn't give up.* The bandits burned his village. He lost the gold. The smoked-fish project failed. The bees got away and stung everyone, *but Uncle Zeka kept trying.* Even if he was falling down a mine shaft—Tapiwa had to choke back tears—he wouldn't give up.

And neither would she.

"Bertha!" Tapiwa shouted over the big woman's moans.

"What is it? Are you hurt?" cried Bertha.

"Uncle Zeka is all right."

"But—but we saw the car fall."

"That's why he's all right. Progress Minister Soso says nothing is stronger than a Mercedes. That's why the government people buy them. They're made for African roads, *and nothing can break them apart!*"

"Do you think so?" said Bertha, loosening her hold.

"Yes! And that's why we have to rescue Uncle Zeka. He's probably sitting down there right now, helping himself to the picnic lunch."

"I hope so," Bertha said. "I made a very nice potato salad."

"You go to the road and stop a farm truck. Get someone to call the police," said Tapiwa. "I'll look for vines and make a rope."

"You're just like him," exclaimed Bertha admiringly. "He always knows what to do." She got up unsteadily. Her dress was torn, and her skin was bruised, but Bertha, now that she had something important to do, began walking back to the road.

Tapiwa found a small stream overgrown with trees and vines. Uncle Zeka had taught her which ones to use for ropes. She hacked them off with sharp stones and braided them together. When she was finished, she ran back to the mine shaft.

She listened. She heard nothing but the wind over the rocks and a faint trickle of the stream. Tapiwa wanted to call down the hole, but she was afraid no one would answer. She tied the vine rope firmly to the stump of the tree growing out of the side of the hole. Then she climbed down.

The rope lasted until she was far below the broken gridwork of branches. She had made it as long as possible, but that wasn't enough. For the first time, Tapiwa realized she had been stupid. She wasn't strong enough to climb back up. The sides of the shaft were crumbling, and worst of all, the rope itself seemed to be slipping. She braced her feet against the stones, but they fell out from under her and she banged against the side.

Then the rope did come loose. With a scream, she slid down, clawing at the rocks. At last, she came to a stop on a heap of gravel at the bottom.

"Who's there?" called Uncle Zeka. She sat up. He was coming along a tunnel with a flashlight.

"Uncle Zeka!" she cried.

"Oh, good! You brought me a rope," he said, picking up the vine.

Tapiwa began to laugh and cry at the same time. "Yes, I b-brought you a rope. It w-was tied to a t-tree. If I'd brought the tree, we'd have s-something to tie it to now."

"Is Bertha looking for help?" asked Uncle Zeka, studying her closely.

"Yes."

"Then it's time for lunch! Come on. I forgot about the picnic in the excitement. Can you walk?"

Tapiwa followed him along the tunnel for a long way. "How did you get so far?" she asked.

"You can go very fast downhill," Uncle Zeka said.

"When the car fell through the grid, I jumped into the driver's seat. *Maiwee!* It was speeding! It's a good thing there weren't any traffic cops. I turned the wheels this way and that to avoid the sides." He showed her how. "When I got to the bottom, I pointed it right up this tunnel. I went on until—but you can see."

Tapiwa could. The car was half-buried in a heap of loose gravel. One headlight was smashed, but the other's beam shone out between two rocks.

"But that's not all!" said Uncle Zeka excitedly. He aimed the flashlight at the top of the gravel. There was a small opening. "I found a huge mine tunnel behind that. It must have been hidden for years."

"Can we have lunch now?" Tapiwa asked in a weak voice.

"Oh, yes, I forgot. You sit down, and I'll look in the trunk."

Tapiwa felt that she couldn't move another inch. The effects of the accident were catching up with her. She wanted to crawl into the car and go to sleep.

Bertha's lunch was scattered around the basket, but some of it was still safely packed in plastic boxes.

"I went through that opening looking for gold," said Uncle Zeka, his mouth full of potato salad.

"It's probably all gone," said Tapiwa. "After all, this is an abandoned mine."

"Not all gone," said Uncle Zeka. He unwrapped a rag and took out a lump of gold as big as her fist.

"Oh-h-h," she sighed.

"It's very heavy. I found it inside the broken headlight." Uncle Zeka laughed heartily.

"You'd better hide it. Progress Minister Soso is sure to claim it," said Tapiwa.

Uncle Zeka winked and wrapped the nugget up again.

"Hello? Hello?" came a voice from behind them. Back toward the hole where Tapiwa and Uncle Zeka had fallen in, flashlights stabbed into the darkness.

"We're here!" Uncle Zeka shouted.

"Are you hurt?" said one of the policemen. "We brought a doctor."

"Look at *that*," said the other, shining his light on the car.

"Ah! Ah!" everyone cried.

"It's in good shape, considering what it's been through," the first policeman said in wonder.

"Amazing!" said the second.

"That's because I was behind the wheel," Uncle Zeka said.

The policemen looked at him in astonishment. "You *drove* this car down the mine shaft and all the way here? You must be the greatest driver in the world."

Uncle Zeka puffed out his chest.

"Do you mind? There's a sick child here," said the doctor, pushing him to one side. He shook his head over Tapiwa's cuts and scratches. "How did you get here? You were supposed to be outside."

"I know one thing," said the first policeman. "He sure isn't going to drive the car *out* again."

For the first time, Uncle Zeka looked upset.

It was past midnight, and only a ghostly half-moon lighted their way. "You shouldn't have come. You're far too weak," Father said in a worried voice.

"I have to say good-bye," said Mother.

"Don't worry. It's only a few more feet." Bertha had her arm around Mother to catch her if she stumbled, and Tapiwa held on to Mother's hand. Tongai followed behind.

They went along the swimming-pool fence to a garden shed where Cuthbert stored tools and tanks of chlorine. A thread of light shone around the door. "It's me," Father whispered into the keyhole.

Cuthbert unbolted the door. "Were you followed?" he said.

"I don't think so. Progress Minister Soso's bodyguards are still parked outside our house. They drank a lot of beer earlier." Father helped Mother into a chair.

Cuthbert rebolted the door. "So this is good-bye," he said to Uncle Zeka, who sat on the floor next to a grain bag full of his belongings. Bertha burst into tears.

"Don't be upset," Uncle Zeka said. "I'm only going away for a while. As soon as I make a lot of money, I'll be back."

"Of course you will," said Mother. She put her hand on Tapiwa's head, and Tapiwa snuggled closer to her chair.

"Can the children come with us?" Uncle Zeka stood up and tied the top of the grain bag shut.

"Tongai can't miss school. Tapiwa, of course, doesn't have that problem," Father said.

"Uh-oh," said Uncle Zeka.

"Aunt Rudo had her removed from Lobatse School." Mother smiled down at Tapiwa, who held on tightly to a wad of Mother's skirt. "Actually, I think Tapiwa will do well in any school. And it won't hurt her to have a vacation."

"Those Lobatse girls are a nest of snakes. *Nyoka!*" said Cuthbert. "They pour sand into the baby pool and pull poor swimmers under to frighten them. I often have to throw them out."

"All they have is a lot of money. They bribe the teachers to get good grades," said Bertha, patting Tapiwa on the shoulder.

"A lot of money is nice," remarked Uncle Zeka, but everybody frowned at him.

Father went outside to be certain Progress Minister Soso's bodyguards weren't around. Uncle Zeka shook hands with Cuthbert. Tapiwa was torn between wanting to stay with Mother and being sure Uncle Zeka got safely to his new home.

"Don't worry," said Bertha to Tapiwa. "I'm going to stay at your house until you get back. I'll cook your mother big meals to be sure she gets nice and fat."

"I'll drive everyone home as soon as you're gone," promised Cuthbert.

Tapiwa smiled a watery smile and let go of Mother's skirt. She followed Uncle Zeka to the door, only looking back once to be sure everything was all right.

They drove through the night—Father, Uncle Zeka, and Tapiwa. Shortly after dawn, they turned off the empty tar road to a bumpy dirt track that sent up a plume of dust behind them. The heat was dreadful, and there were tsetse flies everywhere. They were as big as houseflies and ten times as strong. Tapiwa slapped them hard, but they only bounced off her and came back. Uncle Zeka showed her how to crack them between her fingers.

Then there wasn't even a road. Thorn trees and acacias dotted the landscape, with flat grassland between. Father drove slowly and carefully along old wheel tracks. When he got to a dry stream, he put branches down so the car wouldn't get stuck in sand. He looked very tired. Uncle Zeka offered to drive, and Father was almost rude to him.

At last, they came to the Medical Research Center on the banks of the Rukomeche River. A group of attractive houses with grass roofs were laid out along orderly roads. Large gardens of vegetables and alfalfa were watered by canals. Dr. Chirundu came out to meet them.

Father, Uncle Zeka, and Dr. Chirundu went off on a bush walk, but Tapiwa was left behind in one of the houses. She found a little refrigerator and bottles of cool drinks. Tapiwa drank one, not caring whether she was allowed to or not. Her heart was hot within her.

The time passed slowly. She wondered what was keeping them. Perhaps Dr. Chirundu had been trampled by a rhinoceros. No such luck, Tapiwa thought. He was used to rhinoceroses. He would survive and give Uncle Zeka a job. Then she would never see her uncle again.

At least he had the gold nugget hidden in his grain bag. She remembered the stories he had told her about the gold pieces in Mozambique. She could close her eyes and see everything. She could hear laundry slap on the rocks, babies squeal, and old men snore under shady trees in Uncle Zeka's village. She could smell cook fires, roasting fish, and ripe *marula* fruit in the sun. And that was the story locked into a gold piece the size of a rice grain. What a wonderful tale must be hidden in a nugget the size of her fist!

Dr. Chirundu's voice startled her out of a half sleep. "I can't tell you how delighted I am with your brother Zeka," he said.

"I'm glad you like him," said Father.

"*Like* him? He's the most exciting thing that's happened since I took over the medical school. He knows the names of hundreds of plants. He recognizes every kind of bird, beetle, and ant. His knowledge is fantastic!"

Tapiwa went to the door. Dr. Chirundu was waving his arms, and his glasses bobbed up and down on his nose. "Furthermore," he said, "Zeka knows the *uses* of everything he sees. This is information everyone thought was lost. Our ancestors knew a great deal about medicine, but no one wrote it all down. I didn't think there was anyone left like Zeka. Believe me, the man is a national treasure."

Tapiwa's heart swelled with pride. She was glad Dr. Chirundu hadn't been trampled by a rhinoceros.

"Hello, Tapiwa," Father said. "Are you ready to go?"

"Will we ever come back?" she said.

"Of course! You're always welcome," said Dr. Chirundu. But Tapiwa knew that Father's car was too old to make such a difficult trip again. They walked to the road. The scientists' cars were parked in a row at the side. Uncle Zeka was waiting.

"Good-bye," said Tapiwa, struggling to keep back her tears.

"Good-bye," said Uncle Zeka. "Don't forget. Next time I'm in town, we're going to hunt for gold."

"That won't be for a long time," Dr. Chirundu said. "We plan to keep him busy here." Father looked relieved.

Tapiwa got into the car and watched Father say good-bye to his brother. Then he got in and started the motor.

Uncle Zeka was standing next to a new and expensive-looking Land Rover. He was polishing the mirror with the end of his shirt. "This is a very nice car," he said.

"Thank you," said Dr. Chirundu. "Do you know how to drive?"

But Father drove on before Tapiwa could hear what Uncle Zeka answered.

glossary

SHONA WORDS

baba   (*baa*-baa)   Father. A polite word for older men.

kapenta   (kuh-*pen*-tuh)   Dried, smoked fish.

kaya   (*kai*-yuh)   A small house or shack.

maiwee   (*mai*-wei)   Good grief! My goodness!

marula   (maa-*roo*-luh)   A tree and its yellow fruit, about the size of a small plum. Marulas have four times as much vitamin C as oranges.

mbira   (mm-*bee*-ruh)   A rock rabbit. It looks like a large guinea pig with short hair.

mopane flies (mo-*paa*-nee or mo-*paa*-ne)   Stingless bees that like to drink moisture from eyes, nose, and mouth. They are very irritating.

msasa   (mm-*saa*-saa)   A handsome shade tree with red leaves in the spring. Much of Africa between Kenya and South Africa is covered with msasa trees.

muroyi   (muh-*roy*)   A witch.

muti	(*moo*-tee) Medicine, or a magic potion.
nganga	(nn-*guhng*-guh) A healer or traditional African doctor.
nyoka	(nn-*yo*-kuh) A snake, or snakes.
sadza	(*suhd*-zuh) A stiff cornmeal porridge.
vababa	(vaa-*baa*-baa) Honored father. An extrapolite word for older men.

WORDS FROM OTHER LANGUAGES

Cabora Bassa	(Caa-*bo*-raa *Baa*-saa) This means "the end of the work." Slave traders used to sail up the Zambezi River to capture people. When they got to the Cabora Bassa rapids, they couldn't travel any farther. They named the area "the end of the work." This is a Mozambiquan word.
civet cat	(*si*-vet) English name for a medium-sized carnivore related to the mongoose. It is not a true cat. It has shaggy, gray fur with black spots and black rings on the tail.
mealie	(*mee*-lee) English word for corn.
vlei	(flei) Afrikaans word for marshy wasteland. The Shona word is *bani* (*baa*-nee), but vlei is commonly used.

PLACE NAMES AND PROPER NAMES

Dr. Chirundu	(Chee-*roon*-doo)
Harare	(Haa-*raa*-rei or Huh-*raa*-ree)
Lobatse School	(Lo-*baat*-sei)
Mr. Magadza	(Muh-*guhd*-zuh)
Mozambique	(Mo-saam-*beek*. English speakers say Mo-zam-*beek*.)
Mufakose	(Moo-fuh-*ko*-se)
Rukomeche River	(Roo-*ko*-me-che)
Aunt Rudo	(*Roo*-do)

Sengerera Hills	(Sein-gei-*rei*-raa)
Tapiwa	(Taa-*pee*-waa)
Tongai	(Tong-*gai*)
Zambezi River	(Zaam-*bei*-ze or Zaam-*bei*-zee. English speakers say Zam-*bee*-zee.)
Uncle Zeka	(*Zei*-kuh. Mozambiquans would say *Sei*-kaa.)
Zimbabwe	(Zeem-*baab*-wei)

PRONUNCIATION GUIDE

Symbol	English Word Containing the Correct Sound
aa	mama
a	cat
ai	eye
e	pen
ei	egg
ee	feet
i	hit
o	note
oo	boot
oy	boy
uh	up